T0082755

Brian Miller:
DRAGON-STARS AT WAR

Brian Miller:
DRAGON-STARS AT WAR

BOOK EIGHT

J. MICHAEL BROWER

BRIAN MILLER: DRAGON-STARS AT WAR
BOOK EIGHT

This is a work of fiction. All of the characters, names, incidents, organizations, and dialogue in this novel are either the products of the author's imagination or are used fictitiously.

iUniverse books may be ordered through booksellers or by contacting:

iUniverse
1663 Liberty Drive
Bloomington, IN 47403
www.iuniverse.com
844-349-9409

With illustrations or photos by: Rachel Genevieve Fort

ISBN: 978-1-6632-1305-1 (sc)
ISBN: 978-1-6632-1306-8 (e)

Print information available on the last page.

iUniverse rev. date: 11/05/2020

ACKNOWLEDGEMENT

This is for Michael French, my friend

"Do you fear the force of the wind,
The slash of the rain?
Go face them and fight them,
Be savage again."
—Hamlin Garland, "Do You Fear the Wind?"

"You have to be determined to change the world with your film,
even though nothing changes." —Hayao Miyazaki

"If you're afraid of getting a rotten apple, don't go to the barrel,
get it off the tree!"—Sean Connery, The Untouchables

"Science is nothing but a piece of trash,
before a profound dream" —Paprika

Song from Billie Eilish "Everything I
Wanted" gratefully acknowledged.

Wikipedia: The Free Encyclopedia, gratefully acknowledged for the picture providing lightning and electrical-discharge phenomena and football positions. Song, "Close to You," by Karen Carpenter, gratefully acknowledged.

CONTENTS

— CHAPTER HYPER-ZERO —
SOREIDIAN ULTIMATUM

—YOU*CAN'T*WIN!!! AND I'VE HAD ENOUGH OF ALL THIS Brian-Miller-made-human-shit!!!

And milli-seconds later, on a bright summer morning, in my second-floor office, my massive Australian iron-oak door was brutally kicked in. This powerful forward-recall penetrated the whole structure. The iron-oak door flew literally off its hinges. My hapless desk, the agonizing victim, was literally thrown out my window like it was hit by a massive locomotive. The door crumbled and split into two halves, I could see at least that much, before it littered the lawn outside. Every bit of thunder crashed into my giant, but utterly forlorn, office as a happenstance.

Fortunately, the attentive, ever-watchful female Black World sword set up a defensive screen around me. This whisking-me-away was key to my safety behind her brave blade, she set me outside the reptilian-borne carnage. All this just as we were two steps away from leaving Earth, seeing our last sunset for all companions.

My Black World Sword carried me away from assured death. This was just routine for her, dealing with saurians and all. She was used to sudden things happening, like a dragon crashing through my roof, for instance. Since my desk was thrown out my oversized, vast office, she thought it was all matter of course.

If some human 'had enough,' it wouldn't have amounted to really anything. Even a benign or enlightened 'dictator' like Putin or Kim Jung Un would seek counsel if they ever had (politically) enough, they'd see what others thought, nominally. Not so for a pure reptilian anarchist. They can't (not 'don't') care what the world thinks. The Earth would keep spinning around it's nonexistent top, but dragons would act.

Soreidian just went on ranting to no one and anyone. He was disappointed that kicking my door in wasn't the death of me. The other saurians were frozen and, I'm afraid, listening, too.

—And I'm not taking any more of Brian's stinking feces! Where'd that miserable, smarmy, hillbilly brat disappear to? Oh, there you are, Brian Miller Human, cowering behind your petty, nuisance Black World blade? If I could get you, silly-witch-sword, in my ghostly claws, I'd end your brain in an instant! You whiny weapons are the real salvation of humanity, and they do need salvation, don't they? And you came to this world in association with us, and you've befriended the companions, same as with Tiperia! Adults are corruption incarnate, but you adorable teenagers have convinced the gods that humanity isn't hopeless. You're a virus, and you are the leader, don't deny it. The very fact that you ascended to this repugnant hypergamy in our esteemed saurian ranks is a total, absolute outrage. And I'm an anarchist, talking like this to you. I'd lock you up in Antananarivo Prison in Madagascar forever, the injustice you need. That's what is appropriate for you: Fleas, roaches, lice, the Black Death and everything of natural designs to plague you forevermore. Just smell the dumb and the scallywhops on Brian, everyone! Jason and Rachel are the exceptions, the rest, I'm just so ready to leave, and I've paid back the Russians for their help during the Twins of Triton event, too. And don't play your silly little gender and race thingy on me, Brian: we have, what, seven or eight "non-whites" that are companions. Know this: these "none Caucasian people," or whatever politically-neutered thing you're saying these days, there was no 'angry clowning around here' in picking them, and they aren't fruit off the tree, either. We don't play that color-line or that race-thing. Thing is, if the white race just 'gave up' to the 'colored' races, what kind of a mercy will be shown? Like none, because of all the white-slavery-shit that's gone on in the past. The saurians looked for perfection. They found it, and that's enough said. I know all about your secret plan with Katrina and Teresia were they went back in time, and now you have 5,000 dragons right in your solar system, right here, what, to prevent nuclear war on your insignificant Earth? And you think they will companion with humans in the end? Remember in war everything is possible and a real hero is either a drunk or an idiot, and you are a lickspittle with a stupid dragon companion on your simple side. Wysteria is the 'replacement' for Pluto, right, only a whole lot closer to Earth? Your connivance doesn't stop here, you've secret designs to get Black World swords treasure hunting on sunken ships? What a total outrage! You'll have these witless Black World weapons bringing you Flint's Gold, I can see Long John Silver's ghost arising from Davy Jones' Locker! I just can't believe the mischief you get up to, and around dragon-stars, no less, I thought your ridiculous wives could reign you in. Remember, you can't get away from your DNA! These are just a few of the reasons why I'm trying to end you.

I busted out instinctively.

—It wasn't me your Lordship, you've got it so wrong, and, with the Wysterian's god-like power, well, they had to put the planet somewhere so why not here in our local neighborhood, we have plenty of room, geez. Bargaining with God for what I could get? I made a deal with a small 'g' god, and so what? Wysteria is just before Mars, and it's a tad hotter there. You'd have to speak to the Wysterian and Katrina as to how they did all this, that's got nothing to do with me. I just gave it a little, you know, impetuous encouragement, that's all. The gravity and bullshit will be the same, so what's the harm, I wouldn't make any big deal out of it. And your blaming me for just that? I was wondering if the swords could actually find those trillions of dollars' worth of treasure, and so what? I was just playin' and I didn't think they'd take me so seriously. It's not like I was thinking of paying the whole U.S. national debt off with this just-found wealth, goodness no, or at least not right away! Speaking of debt, your breath is smelling a little manky again, what have you been up to? Why do I always get the blame for saurian decisions, why are you foisting all this on me? Our kindly Black-World weapons looking for treasure island in their off-time, and these random thoughts *thought* everywhere, and just so <u>what</u> is the <u>what</u> to all this?

Soreidian just continued, so imperiously.

—And that's why I'm here to end it, Brian Miller Human, all this intervention on Earth, and all this trouble starts with you.

Soreidian, of course, was a dragon, a star-dragon, a dragon-star, power-extensive to literally crush, squash and squish the entire Earth into a literal spitball and that promptly. Don't test this Alpha (and Omega) male, seriously don't.

The raging reptilian didn't anticipate the amount of saurians and teenage companions in my vast workplace. My office was filled to the brim and over it, in terms of attendance like that day on Lincoln Beach when I went for a wild ride in Soreidian's version of Apocalypse Before, Current and After.

Littorian, however, wasn't having any of it. My companion violently arose from his Sphinx position, massive muscles raging, not caring that my office was one-half in the breeze, glass spread wide over the manicured lawn. The Lord of the Lizardanians had his own, personal agenda.

All the other saurians were silent, and that included Larascena, too. She mentally summoned out of the carnage the diamond she created from the Water World, holding it up for me to see, winking. Everything else, was out on the glass-reigned-grass, but not this, not my diamond. Then Littorian spoke.

4

—I want, I desire, I plead, I demand, and I really <u>need</u> a sparring match with you, Soreidian, and there is nothing that can prevent it. Nothing! I'm so sick of this dorky dictatorship and your mush-mouthed-hack- companions, just smirking behind you. This spot-treatment of Brian is unjustified, I can't stand it anymore. So, let's just have an end to it, me and you it's war!

That look of finality really took me aback. I looked at my companion like I didn't even know him. Did a little sparring match overcome my friendship with Littorian? It couldn't be so. Admittedly, this friendship was only a few months old, and sparring matches were a necessity in saurian history for many eons. My options were fading quickly, as Soreidian's unregulated monologue continued.

—Yes, all wars are just a matter of spilling the guts out of selected soldiers, and maybe that makes dragons just the same as our erstwhile hosts. Shit-illy granted. As though humans had the god-like 'right' to host anyone on this planet. Yes, I've learned their silly capitalism, socialism, limited-anarchism and communism and always and everywhere, they can't accomplish the lofty, only what is degenerately sewer ridden. Limbo, lust, gluttony, greed, anger, heresy, violence, fraud, treachery all adding up to Lucifer, yes, I've read Dante, and I find it really heinous, all these silly syllogisms. You can't 'teach' anyone different, unless they're a teenager, that's the highest point to get them to understand something dissimilar. Similarly, you can't be a 'genius intellectual' and a capitalist. Capitalism follows human nature, and that is limited, so, limited capitalism, the need to shake down someone's pants. And you're a dumb saurian shit, Littorian! You can't save anything by 'giving' it to mankind! Only the teenagers, there's a little hope. We can adjust their DNA, RNA and whatever else, that's as far as gods go, though. Even you, arrogant Brian, know this much: Freedom of speech doesn't apply when you're dealing with national sovereignty and socialization, on the Earth, now days: any fool can see that. It's all an avalanche of absurdism, but it's our avalanche and I threw the snowball. If you give humans something, they will want everything that's just their way, time limited creatures, these! You know that no revolution is possible without a good dose of terrorism; and terrorism is the mask of death, the only ones that can kill you <u>are</u> <u>other people</u> (pandemic be shit-damned). If mankind were squirrels, maybe they'd bury nuts for a rainy day, but they are just humans, they can't save anything, even if you hand it to them. And all this avarice I've just mentioned? I think teenagers are the answer, only a dragon can make it last for forever and a day. Littorian, I'd love to have a sparring match with you. If it culminates in your death, so be it. You stinking, miserable worm, I just need to know immediately <u>where</u> and <u>when</u>?

I burst in, as was my wont.

—I think that no reptilian here will support a sparring match between Littorian and Soreidian. You're just generalizing about mankind and you are no general to me or anybody with sense. It honestly doesn't mind me, and I'm sure no one wants y'all to fight, right, isn't that true everybody?

…and right into a gigantic, fly-spotted horse pile.

I completely overestimated my chances as to any kind of 'saurian reason.' Talk about a humiliating deflation and round-a-bout defeat!

All the saurians were aghast, and there was a murmuring growl from every reptilian. All except one: Kerok. Nothing ever seemed to surprise him, and he just snickered to himself and thought to me:

Oh, my human, you'll never learn, but hopefully as a nascent teenage dragon-star, well, maybe that will cure you, we'll see!

Larascena spoke for everyone.

—I think <u>not</u>, Brian Miller! Just say no to the teenager-toddler inside of you. Are you outside of your tinctured mind? Every dragon-star-one-of-us want this sparring match! I've no time to consider your hurt feeling spread all over the lawn like your vast window-esque! A saurian respects honor and dignity—if they are defended with a pure heart and power, sex, and entertainment trump everything and anything. That would be just the thing to end this war completely. That will put a pretty little flower on our general saurian departure from Earth. Not sure what 'arrangement' you've got with Katrina, Teresian and their time-travel fetish, and I certainly don't care. This will be like Genotdelian's removal, who wouldn't celebrate that? Yeah, I've got the mental images, but it's better to have a front row Sphinx position for it all! I'd have loved to be there on Neptune to see the happy end (as in saurian-kicked-butt) of the Lord of the Crocodilians. Who knows, maybe Soreidian might win when they spar? Fun times! And if Soreidian wins, well, I'm willing to be overcharged for my seat. I'm not sure, as Clare is hinting as an aside to me, that you are the monster here, Brian Miller, but we will see!

I whispered to my steel-ultra-Velociraptor, prudently, of course.

—Wow, you hit me right in my saurian-feels, my lady. You are condemning me to drive my request for reconsideration on and on until my wheels are worn to nothing and I've come to the edge, and the end, and the abyss, of the world, is that what you want? All my levity fails like a just-popped, oversized and jizzy zit. Tiperia said that Littorian shouldn't spar with Soreidian because, has they say, 'hope remains to be seen,' and because then he'd be—

Lara raised her seven-inch index claw imperiously.

—Don't care, don't give one tiny shit, my petulant but well-meaning-rabbit-and-rabid-human. I'm monstrously vilifying you, shut your piehole! Excuse me, excuse me? Oh, I really don't give one hooey, sit-the-bench with all your imbecilities! The real people are speaking, sit by your dumb dish. Hope is what "remains to be seen"? What a stupid statement that is, which confirms that all writing is indeed a mule-pack of lies. Remains? Hope has remains, I guess? Stupid and dumb. And "to be seen?" 'Hope' is seen? Like you can see 'hope'? Even if it's all allegorical and somehow symbolic, it's an exercise into the total ridiculous-shame-bolic, you are so full of fanfaronade arrogance, this sparring will be epic and super, I can't wait; and I will be there to see this event between Littorian and Soreidian! Punishment of the-here, won't reflect on your suffering-on-the-'morrow. Remember, as Chico Marx said, You gonna believe me or your lying eyes? Just as a for-instance, I was studying this

'Precariat,' the "precarious proletariat": For me, that means when the workers develop bourgeois tendencies and human-fanciful-likes, making them shift in their social positions, that is, they don't want to be workers anymore but will take the bourgeoisie existence, just to erode the castle of the proletariat, down to the welcome and inviting ground. People are peasants, they need to possess whatever it is. They have no "higher conscience." That's what I think of your workers, they are just nascent bourgeoisie. You can't have 'conversations' to 'remove' racism or any other -ism, you need to change the DNA, and yes, I'm talking about throwing the baby out with the bathwater, and just go-dragon, ripping out all that nuisance human DNA bullshit. You need muscle, not water, dummy! That's the way to fix stuff, but good. Just thought to add that in, seeing as how I'm making a grand-saurian speech. That's what I think workers are: Desiccant, disguised (and deceitful) middle-class-just-wanting, like Americans, to be 'rich' one day. You see, I'm trying to make this a calm normalcy just before our running-for-the-door departure. All you have to do is get humans talking, then you see the contradictions, but when saurians speak, it's not so. Let's not interfere with this grand adventure in top-sparring! Just so!

At this affront I didn't know what to say (and this is again, my aggravating wont).

—I can't believe the saurian position on this, it's unbelievable.

Clare chimed in, throwing up her extremely gorgeous, scaled and muscular arms.

—There isn't a 'saurian position on this,' that cries against anarchy, my creamy dual-husband prude-ski. And sure, it's unbelievable to a mere child imitating a pre-dragon-teenager, and I'm finin' to spank a half-moon soon, silly husband! After all, the ends (as in human butt-ends) justify the means, if they are anarchical-saurian ends! I'm not going 'aggro,' I'm going for 'satisfaction,' or just 'sat'! I love this, all this sobriquet- ting, abusing all the words down to their raw essence, just like gangster rap.

Clare laughed hysterically. Larascena, too, stretched her built-shoulders out and did a little-muscle check all around. She knew that this excited me, and I confess it did.

—You're still in anarchy elementary school, my silly, benighted dual-husband. This is brainstorming not brain drizzling, you-silly-silly. Hey, I didn't hear the marble move around in your miniscule head, let me move it around a little, okay? Brian, done educate yourself! Dragons need to spar; don't you know anything? And it's okay, I understand your misbehavin', I'm just here to rein you in, and I'll take the other benighted-half-moon, Clare.

CHAPTER ZERO
EPIC OF EPICOSITY

AT WITS-END-AND-OVER-IT, IN WALKED JOAN OF ARC. HER HANDS raised like she was calling all of Heaven to her saving aid.

—Wait just a saurian minute! I'm not God's spokeswoman for nothing, Christ please every-one of my grand reptilians; can you listen, late in this day with me? Before our needed ferocity, let's play a game!

Of the companions, all were silent, waiting to see what would happen. The saurians were all listening too, even the irate Soreidian and his partner Danillia[1].

---

[1] Danillia needs no introduction. In this case, I'll make an exception. Ever since I came across her in Vermont, when she was shape-shifted into Leah Starblue, she has had it in for me. My first-sight of her was a good indication of her hidden cruelty, here it is, from <u>Brian Miller and the Twins of Triton</u> and this is narrated by Katrina: Ms. Starblue walked in and what a wild sight she was, even for fashion-crippled Vermont! Her clothes were from someone's attic corner. Easily six feet tall and somewhat stooped over, the woman regarded the class with a slightly worried look, as though she had never seen so many kids in one place together. It was the look of someone unsure of whether they should take the last cookie on the plate. Then it's gone. She had the look of a

—In other words, my gentle ultra-dinosaurs, trust me. Littorian wants to kill, Soreidian wants to kill. Nothing can stop that sentiment. Alright. First, football. Then, Littorian and Soreidian can spar-to-death. Of the companions, the leading females will quarterback, the males will kick. And that means all the raw, physical action will be with dragons alone. The location is in Portland, Oregon, and I'm sure Soreidian and Littorian know that place well, God please you. You had a trial there, if I have it right from Brian? Simple, by God's rights, right?

Then the Maid winked at the open-mouthed saurians.

Joan decidedly rescued me. Good thing Joan was there to take over, I was walking point and I got clobbered and purposefully shitted on (even though real saurians, meaning dragon-stars, don't).

---

parent trying to park the car and losing their nerve. The spot goes to another driver. It's a kind of hesitancy that a kid can't help but love to see. She could have been in her 40s or 60s, it was hard to tell. She was conservatively dressed, but her clothes seemed better suited for another era—the blouse was a plaid, as in rhyming with 'bad', Brian says, (and not the good kind of bad, either, just YUCK!). Her hair was long, but pulled back, severely tied with nothing more than a piece of ribbon—odd looking, cheap ribbon. Impossible to say exactly what color the single piece of material was, it fluttered and seemed to change its shade as the wearer moved, but slowly, subtly, like a flower opening its petals or seaweed undulating on the ocean floor. Wearing a plaid blouse, of course, she was nervous—definitely cruel (and I know it!). She wore no glasses, but looked like she should have, for her eyes had the crow's feet of extreme study. Her eyes were light green with a very pale blue line about the iris. The eyes flashed about. I thought she was wearing those gaudy contact lenses that messed up eye color. Her gaze was not friendly. The lips, thin, were not curved in anything like a smile. This student teacher wasn't looking to make nice with us.

The room hushed, not a whisper. The woman was still looking around the room. Then she saw me. And at that moment, a slight smile did appear—but only for a second, and it was more of a smirk than anything else. She looked me up and down quickly and then actually tossed her head! I think she wanted to insult me. Now, I'm sure of it. Then she saw Brian and gave him a crooked, mean-girl little grin that lasted longer, and ended in a sneer.

I think I should say this now, because where, but through writing, would I be induced to say it? Saurians eat a lot, that's true, and its vast ocean food, but as far as 'Number 2' is concerned, they have power to 'defer' that unpleasant aspect of things, by neutralizing and dissipating 'the whole affair.' That includes number one, by the way. Later, I witnessed how they did it. Wow, enough said, really bigly. Oh, this isn't any type of foreshadowing. Alright, it is. Anyway, that's not important right now. In attendance (and with a slack-jawed, golf-ball-o'-face look at the sizeable destruction of my office) were Sheeta Miyazaki, Joan of Arc, Jing Chang, Nausicaa Lee, Robert Fisher, Katrina Ivanonva Chakiaya, Jason Shireman, Rachel Dreadnought, Ivan Chakiaya, Alexandra, Natalya, and little Darcey. Everyone was present because we were discussing leaving Earth and then, of a sudden, calamity-mine-time!

I weakly looked to Katrina, because I was so lost, just then. This companion I was exceedingly close to, she silently mouthed this to me:

NYET.

And that was what I most needed to hear then. Yes, when your friend is down, kick him in the face, that's the way-it-is. I really couldn't blame her, you know.

She's Russian, capeesh?

At once, I felt so alone, no one, saurian or human was with me. Maybe Kerok was, but he's so complicated, and he knew well of saurian traditions. I thought maybe I had a problem with just me. I could always (and everywhere) turn to my companion, Littorian, he could comfort me, guide my struggling mind to where it ought to be. My dragon could do this, but not this time. I frowned to myself, and thought, if I didn't have a stroke, I could bring the saurians around. I was cured of my stroke, but I thought that something was lacking, not convincing them to turn the other masseter muscle. What a human indictment.

I was glad Joan was there to take over. Leading the companions was a natural place for this Maid of Orleans. She arrived just in time, which was my concealed desire. I'd been in charge too long. This was the finish for me as 'leader' of the companions, and a good thing too.

Joan and Tiperia had a secret agreement unknown to anyone. Yes, Jeannette knew what to do.

—Let me be frank, my glorious reptilians. You have saved me, and I'm grateful for this, but you are in some conflict here. I'm God's messenger, and I have a ready-made solution for you to consider, my dragons. You want to have a sparring match Littorian and Soreidian. All right. No human, having sense, would oppose this. Littorian's companion we can just set aside, Brian's talking like a 'common-ist' again, in a well-meaning way. Anyone knows that Communism is strong when people's faith is lessened just because people aren't dragons; if they were, they'd go for anarchy. Simple as Marionberry Pie. We delayed stopping Time to go after the Donner Party, right, my pet-peeve? You see, I've learned. Therefore, and ergo, I think a football game should be first, then spar, that'd be just the thing. If everyone agrees that we should play a little game before the big fight, then everyone will have a chance to fight saurians on either side of this issue. Saint's preserve us, that's just the thing we need before we all go off to the stars. And it's a spiritual dress rehearsal for the sparring match between Littorian and Soreidian that will follow hard upon. What could be better? And when Soreidian wins, that will be the end of Brian Miller (or it better be). That would be Brian's fate, none can avoid it. If you want business-oriented class consciousness, getting back to my time with YouTube, see Requiem for the American Dream, and anyone seeing that film would definitely want a dragon ride or just assume their petty fate to men in white coats. Brian got me going on Youtube.com and now I'm even more of a military genius writ large. Words, however, mean 'who said it,' not 'what' was said. And that is the indictment of all humanity, whether a general, a politician or a day porter and writer, it's all contacts with humans, or, in this case, saurians. So, my honored reptilians, can we play a game first?

Meanwhile, a side meeting was taking place.

Rachel Dreadnought confronted Katrina and got right in her personal space. Katrina turned around, and the teenager had her blond hair in her playful hands, bunches of it. Rachel giggled. Kat jerked her head violently back, and Rachel, nevertheless, tugged and yanked on Katrina's locks.

—So, you're Katrina, huh? Like the storm?

Katrina smiled shortly, successfully getting free of the forced-fondling.

—Like the hurricane, my notable nemesis.

—Ah-huh. Shall we be like sisters, instead, in our little football event?

—Interesting concept. And I like you right off, but just listen. Funny thing and strangely enough, letting you stroke my hair. As you might know if paying attention, I don't wait on people. And I'm so much stronger than that hurricane, so be good, for evening will come; in the night, in the dark: Don't make me end you.

Rachel responded in a spirited way.

—You think you were responsible for that calamity, but don't make me laugh. And I like <u>you</u> right off, too, isn't that grand, but just listen. See, game recognize game? I'd always wanted a Russian storm to defeat, gee I can't wait to get you out on that field. And for Christ's sakes <u>smile</u>, you walking doom-merchant-storm-buggerer! One of us must go down; who's gonna get their throat slllllitttttttttt?

—Well, feel free, errant douchebag.

Rachel got a nasty look, like a witch-found-out.

—I'm going to enjoy this, beating the shit out of you.

This will be more fun than urinating in your French Fries. Oh, but your trying to be American now: Freedom Piss Fries?

Katrina's companion came over.

—Problems here, my human teenagers?

Rachel brightened up, on cue.

—I can sorta certify on that much, my lady, she micro-aggressed me.

Teresian recoiled, made a dragon-star harrumph, just the way a Wysterian should.

—Well, don't be so minuscule-aggressive Katrina, for shame. Have some cordiality when dealing with 'the other side,' if you humanly will, what's come over you, well! If you've an issue with Rachel, let's be done with it on the football field, this will be fun, yes? No?

Rachel beamed, started to depart, waiving in a passionate, air-caress.

—Oh, yes, Teresa, I just can't wait! See ya, Kat, and watch your frightened fries!

The Black World sword took immediate action, and that in a non-political way. The weapons could do football, really so! They universally pleaded to the reptilians not to interfere with whatever 'goings-on' occurred, too. That was done grudgingly, at Tiperia's behest. The swords knew Tiperia's plan, too, selected swords. Tiperia didn't want the two top Lizardanians to fight, it would be like the United States and Russia having a nuclear war. Maybe the US would win, but the results would be decimation, any fool can see that.

For me, I set up a video room with all the deaths, injuries, and the most savage moments of NFL football. This extreme horror show could doubtless impress all saurians to be cautious out on the field. I thought, and this was my second or third mistake (but who's counting?), that caution would ensue all around. Wrong again, it had the opposite reward! Once, when a defensive player was brutally body-slamming a runner, all the saurians were salivating bigly. They powered up strongly and enthusiastically, raring to conquer. The furniture in the room was of course all broken in celebration. Oriasel was overjoyed and nudged Azzaian.

—Did you hear that commentator, there? He said 10 or 15 years ago you could do that in the NFL, lift, crush and crash down an opponent to a sloppy mess? Then the ref said, 'the defender was just overpowered!' That's why you didn't see a flag on the play. You can bet your front seat in hell I'ma do that—and give my saurian such a crater to crawl like a worm out of, yeah, I can't wait to conquer some butt!

All the potential players asked if taunting, unsportsmanlike conduct, jeers, abusive language, aggressive fighting, peel-back blocks, and a row of other matters would generate a flag on the part of the Black World swords officiating the game. That was just after "NFL Best Fights and Ejections 2019-2020". We companions were relaxed, thinking flags would be thrown. That was not in 'anarchy's ken'.

—Unless it's against a vulnerable human. We can't let humans be killed. After all, they are almost 80% water, and what is left is a semi-sentient cricket mallet, meaning their fragile bones, laughable brains and other miscellaneous, troublesome goo. They are very delicate especially for distance/space/time travel. Very challenging for a Black World weapon to handle. If a dragon is outright killed during this 'extended sparring match,' well, then, that's another matter, I think a god can take it, short of a full-tilt add-nauseum Malay. If you mess with a Black World sword official, if you don't follow our 'loose rules' we won't strike you down, but you'll be ejected from the game, it's shower time for you. Don't expect to see many flags thrown during this game: This is saurian time, not sword time.

There was cheering all around for that comment, by the saurians. All the companions wearing the mankind-design looked totally shocked. And it just when down-hill from there.

I just had this to say.

—Wow, it's just so nice to be loved.

Blocks using the helmet were out, too: The dragon-stars needed no helmets. Both Katrina and I took a shallow, gawking look, blinking, and thinking.

What in the world's-fuck did you get us into?

Me? You have me confused with someone else. It was Joan of Arc, she's got helping people all baked in!

She's exempted. It was <u>you</u> showing her a football game, on Youtube. com and stuff. You ridiculous cumdumpster, you showed her the LFL, with those skimpy chicks running around in bikinis, and then the National Football League, too, why'd you do that? You know what LFL means, dummy: Lingerie Football League!

Oh, quit carrying on, Kat! It was named later as the Legends Football League, thank you very much. That's Gridiron football, right, I think that's the official name?

Gridiron? They saurians will be showing up and bending and crushing steel-iron, bronze-iron, and bending anything else of iron when they play and we fragile humans have to cope with it? You've entered us into an arm-breaking meat grinder. They will be thinking this is a giant sparring match, they're triple-inducement to play, that's for sure.

You heard the reptilians; this is what they want, who can argue with that?

And you manipulate things, like you always have, Brian.

Manipulate in a good way and damn you've developed a filthy-ass mouth in this precious few months and that just when we are leaving the Earth entire!

Brian, you should think before you act. Oh, I'm sorry, I didn't swear: You should think before you act, dumb fuck, these are dragons here, don't you know anything?

Joan's to blame, Katrina.

And you're to blame for Joan!

OMG, remember that truth is temporary, and becomes contradictory (at best), and when Joan of Arc is a witch (the truth in 1431) but a Saint (the truth in 1920), see the contradiction? The truth is dependent on Time. Your calling me a Dr. Frankenstein, right? Well, I don't really resent that. My general importance is being overemphasized and exaggerated and what would your Mom say after such sailor's language, Kat?

We ended the irate telepathy right there. The saurians were happy so I'm in the right place. Ipso facto.

CHAPTER ONE

QUARTER ONE

HOWARD GRIFFORD: GOOD EVENING FROM THE PETER W. Stott Community Field, where a war is going on between saurians and humanity has front row seat for your radio pleasure. And that's a great thing that mankind is just a spectator. That's because humans going up against dragons, well, I don't want the clean-up. We'll have all the action on radio at 91.5FM and I don't know if someone will be here with cameras in the crowd, but I wouldn't doubt it. Everyone's got a cell phone, no worries there. Our officials for this event have taken care of all the logistics: the stadium in Portland, Oregon, at the Portland State University all-purpose field, your commentators, radio production, just everything! With me is Frank Facenda, John Maddenhawk and, with sideline reporting, Maddy Kingston, we have on-line a juggernaut of a dragon game to report to you tonight. In fact, we are the only people out here right now, just the Black World weapons and the four of us. Attentive weapons have borrowed bleachers from the basketball court and 5,000 seats are available. The engineering abilities of these Black World weapons I've never seen before, and in so quick a time. Normally for a National Football

League game you'd have 60,000 or 70,000 seats, but we will have to make do, I guess. Already, the seats are filling up, and we have about an hour to kick-off time. The buildings around us, too, are gorging with fans (short for "fanatics" just by-the-way). The Black World weapons are going really Manson with all of this provided free popcorn, hot dogs, wine, beer, and making the visual effects very pleasing to the people. Oh, I think friends of saurians are watching, the Seree, Orcharia and Parcharia have sent three or four people to witness this, too. These aliens are being catered to like royalty, by the well-meaning weapons. Getting back to field-matters, the way to tell 'who is who' is not the verdant green design on the fins of Littorian's team, nor harsh black painted on the sharp blades of Soreidian's side, but the _colors_ of the dragons themselves. That's the way we will tell the individuals apart, very good for all of us. Some of those designs are really striking, too. And much of the colors give the illusion that the muscles are growing! The colors on the saurians are so striking and vibrant, we can easily tell who is who tonight. The lighting is truly excellent, bravo to the engineering skills of the Black World weapons. And the blades, the fins on the dragons are as sharp as serrated steak knives, and I'm expecting some extreme injuries here, you guys. The military folks will have their notebooks out too. Even with a Rod from God and a nuclear weapon for—

MADDY KINGSTON: Hey, what's a Rod from God?

GRIFFORD: It's like a kinetic bombardment using a tungsten rod, okay? Learn a book, geez! It's in <u>A Dragon-Star Lives Forever (More)</u>! So, can I go on? ...a certain Wysterian, will be watched closely, I'm already seeing some generals and admirals arriving. I think they'd be better off injuring Superman than this Wysterian, goodness, she's iron-packed with raw, superlative, corded-muscle. Thank goodness the saurians will confine their ultra-monster punches to fellow reptilians. Kukulkan and Teresian will be spectators because otherwise Soreidian won't participate in the football special. I think he knows the incredible power of those two, and they favor the Green Fins. This doesn't sit right with Teresian because her companion will be quarterbacking for Littorian's team. Katrina insists that the two Wysterians sit-the-bench on the sidelines and watch. So, they compromised. If a Green Fins member is seriously hurt, Teresian will substitute. Soreidian said this would be permissible. The only thing that can bring a saurian down is a Black World weapon or another saurian, quiet obviously. These reptilians love sparring matches, and sometimes they are to the death. They want to leave, but, I guess, the companions are due some favors first. Here's the list, Littorian's NFL Team, the Green Fins: Ettoros, Direidian, Loridian, Terminus, Katrina Ivanonva Chakiaya, Korillia, Littorian, Turinian, Larascena, Clareina, Anakimian with their coach, Kerok. And from the Black Fins, we have Soreidian's NFL Team: Valacian, Oriasel, Verrierian, Saleosian, Uzzaious, Soreidian, Penemuelian, Rachel Dreadnought, Azzaian, Buneian, Danillia, with Rahabian, as the Black Fins coach. The companions have done their share to curtail these bloody contests, but they go on anyway, and the teenage human companions are trod under a saurian iron heel, as a result. I think Maddy has no one to interview, just wandering around the sidelines, waiting for the dragons to arrive. Hey, Maddy, did you arrive okay? These reptilians are sure bringing their own *backpfeifengesicht*, aren't they?

MADDY KINGSTON: *Backpfeifengesicht*? My German is a little weak, that means Howie?

GRIFFORD: It means 'A face in need of punching'.

KINGSTON: Thanks for that, I'll forget it right away, but I bet the saurians will remind me a little bit later. Hello, Howard, and what a story! This six-foot black sword whisked me into my car, spoke exceedingly nicely but insistently, got underneath my Mazda, put an atmosphere over my car, and hurled me from Elizabeth, New Jersey all the way to Portland, Oregon in about a minute. I couldn't believe the sword could lift so much, but I'm not around magic every-other-day, and I looked out my window and I thought I was that car plummeting down to Earth, remember that sports car launched from the Space Shuttle, from *Heavy Metal* have you ever seen that anime?

HOWARD GRIFFORD: That what, Maddy? What's an anime?

KINGSTON: Oh, don't you have kids? Oh, I mean teenagers (a very different animal)? Anime means animation Howard. Heavy Metal was a little harder-hitting, done by another bunch of artists, but my teens liked <u>Castle in the Sky</u>, <u>Nausicaa and the Valley of the Wind</u>, <u>Princess Mononoke</u> and so many others by Hayao Miyazaki, you see? Oh, forget it, my kids used to watch those animation movies. Oh, yes, yes, interview, interview, come here my shy, six-foot little rapier. I'm interviewing the Black World sword that belongs to Brian Miller. Wow, you've got pieces and parts sorta not there, how prosaic, right, er, Mr. or Ms. Sword?

BRIAN MILLER'S BLACK WORLD SWORD: I'm a girl, a woman, I guess? Yes, that! I'm a veteran, hence my prosaic-cos-ity. We kinda don't have names, I mean, look at you, you don't even get to select your own names as humans, right? If your parents name you something silly or weird, then that's your name, isn't it, until your old enough to change it to something civilized, right? Anyhow/way, I'm married to Larascena's sword, too. He's just over there, watching us. Let me give a shout-out to my hatchets and knives helping out with the myriad of logistics here today, including popcorn, hotdogs and liquor. And we have loaned out to the fans in buildings surrounding the field our patented binoculars, too. Isn't it neat, a game between the dragon-stars? I understand this has never happened, so perfect place for me, I love new things! I'm helping with officiating the contest, ask me a National Football League question, dare you!

KINGSTON: I'm sure you'll officiate well. Let me start at the top. Dragons. Dragon-Stars. Star-Dragons. What can we expect as players, do they know the rules? Do you anticipate throwing a lot of flags? Who will be the playmakers on Littorian's team? What is the experience level of your quarterback? Are all those outrageous saurian bulbous muscles as hard as iron? Why aren't you answering any of my questions?

BRIAN MILLER'S SWORD: Golly, simmer down, Maddy, I'll answer, I'll answer. Yes, all the dragons know the rules, and physical forms are awesome-ultra-special, to be sure. If they follow them, well, that's another matter, and enforcement will be negligible, meaning flags will be a rarity. If they break the rules around humans, you'll see some flags. If not, probably not, we will not get extreme on the dragons, that's a no. When the whistle blows, the play is over. If there is some continued contact, well, that's to be expected. Look for that kind of lingering problem between Soreidian, Littorian, Danillia and Korillia. They all have notorious rivalries. If a dragon is outright killed, well, so be it. The dragons can speak, play, for themselves, all dragons' are equal playmakers. And I will answer your questions, ask another!

KINGSTON: How will the dragon stars, who are anarchists, that is, no rules apply, deal with Black World swords officiating them?

BRIAN MILLER'S SWORD: We intend to let the dragons be dragons, I don't get to impose discipline on dragon-stars in general, so our concern is not the way dragons play, but defending the humans when saurians clash. That's why we will be raising the resultant power, not letting the power go towards the crowd. This is very important. Dragons mean Power so we need the airplanes, satellites, people's kites, kid's paper airplanes, weather balloons, skydivers, to stay clear of the field for a few hours, like, no matter how high up they are because the swords will send the power skyward, that is, making it blow up, not blow out, see? The Moon better not come around either, or parts might be blown off. I'm serious now. You don't understand 'power' when it comes from the dragon who is mad. Because then humans will literally get 'puffed away' like a cyclone or tornado, you know, blow their bodies up or something, with so much popcorn and gum in their mouths, like a direct hit from a howitzer, yuck! You remember the Civil War when all those civilians wanted a good picnic seat during the first battle of Bull Run? I've read a lot of human history, you know. The civilians became involved too, just running away. The Black World swords are for safety here, not conquest.

JOHN MADDENHAWK: Moving on, I'm blessed to be a commentator at this event. Just a side note, I've checked the 'mystical footballs' before the game, and we have Black World footballs, and I've never seen the like! Seven footballs will be used, and it will be a trick to see those footballs deflated by the dragons. How would you view this event?

KINGSTON: Let's get to the action-package, and that right away. As you know, it will all come down to power-muscling it on the backfield, as Korillia and Uzzaious battle it out in the half and full back positions. Robert Fisher, on the sidelines, is going crazy, not being able to help his companion, Korillia. The two quarterbacks, Katrina and Rachel Dreadnought will have to pass the rock to these players. I understand that the English translation of the names of all these Lizzies happens-back to the Bible and mythical angels if one looks everything up. For instance, Uzzaious might take its' name from Uzza or Uzziel, which means strength of God, if the ancient Jews have it right. See these two on tap for getting touched on first and second down. Korillia has a definite rivalry with Danillia. Danillia will play Cornerback and Wide Receiver, so watch those two go at it. And right now, Maddy is scheduled to talk with Jeannette, let's go right to her.

JOAN OF ARC: That's right, God preserve you (and me!), and I've been a little shy I admit, I'm just trying to make up my 500 years (plus) of history with some advanced learning. I'm getting better, Saint's preserve us. Things are happening so fast, I'm lucky to be companioned to Anakimian, to guide me through. So, I'm still absorbing. No pressure on me! How is my English-too-good?

KINGSTON: It's good enough for me! It's great English, I think we should talk about tonight's game but just one question from your past?

JOAN: Ask away, Christ bless you!

KINGSTON: Thank you, thank you: I don't think any companion has put as much over-drive, over-stimulus, over-thought, and ultra-over-over into any of this as you have. I think everyone believes that we should let Jehanette be Joan of Arc, right? You are Katrina's back-up, right? I understand that the saurians went back in time to get you, sure, I got that book _Joan of Arc and the Dragon-stars_, fully up on that, what an exciting tale, but what was the real deal, did you indeed have a doppelganger?

JOAN: Saint's preserve us, why don't you ask, 'the other maid'?

DARCEY THE MAID: Hello Maddy, yup, it was me. And Joan and I had the same teacher from the Black World teaching us English. I'm Darcey, the other maid, and I've gone from peasant-infested limited life, to death, to life again, so you know I'm with dragon-stars! Also, Beterienna from the Alligatorian world will be here too, backing up anyone who gets injured on Littorian's team. Can I introduce you to Anaphielian, he will be playing wide receiver and cornerback, and he is all-the-way my companion!

ANAPHIELIAN: Hi, Maddy, I snuck up on you, it seems? Just getting into my snake-in-the-grass mode. I mean to arouse my companion, not particularly you.

KINGSTON: Whoof, yes, you did sneak up on me, wow, you're a giant, Percheron-like, towering Velociraptor!

ANAPHIELIAN: I think I'm a little taller than a 'mere' Velociraptor, and a draft horse? Well, I've ruptured the local gym-to-death, but thanks anyway. The chance to spar for three hours, who can resist, right Maddy?

FRANK FACENDA: For me, I was compelled to be here by certain Black World swords making me an offer I couldn't easily refuse, as they stuffed a whole lotta money in my pockets. Hell, I'm not liable to question all of this, it's for interstellar relations, right? The three of us are inside the booth today, and an incredible design it is, made entirely of oak wood, I've never seen the like before. There is no glass on the commentary booth, here, and we can see the fantastic spectacle easily, 40 feet off the ground. I understand that the dragons can only jump up to five feet, then the attentive official swords will throw a flag on the play, and they'll be other restrictions, too, right Howard?

GRIFFORD: That's right, Frank, and look at the tanks and personnel carriers surrounding the Stott Field, wow, where did they get so many tanks? They are three-tall and three-deep, man, nothing can bust outta that!

FACENDA: I understand from the swords they got them out of the junk yards and off military bases from all over the world, Howard. The Black World weapons have seen to all the logistics and will be officiating the game. What are the stakes, as you comprehend it, John? Check out this equipment, they did raid from everywhere, Turkey, Germany, even Russian tanks! Man, I hope they had permission.

MADDENHAWK: Well, I think the tank enclosure is for human protection, Frank, these dragon stars are here for one night only, then they are off to the stars. It's three tanks tall, and two tanks deep. Then you have personnel carriers around all of that. Still, a saurian at full speed could make match sticks out of the barrier, as I understand it from the attentive Black World swords. And you know what? It's time for a game to break-out. That's why there are Black World knives at the 10-yard line outside the barrier, to direct energy up, not out, vertically, not horizontally. The energy could blow you away like a tornado would, but directed up in the air, folks will be safe. Those stadium seats will be overflowing with spectators, and it's lucky we have the National Guard on hand to keep some order. The admission is free, and will be up to capacity, of course. There are even little kids here to see the event, the parents are that sure about their safety. And magic is all around us, to cure the injuries that will surely be there, especially after the game gets going. The buildings around the campus will be overflowing, too. It's a preview to a sparring match between Littorian, Lord of the Lizardanians, and his second and rival Soreidian. After the game is done, these two will go at it, maybe right there on the field itself, in extreme violence like when Genotdelian, Lord of the Crocodilians, went at it with Littorian, you heard about that one, right Frank?

FACENDA: Yes, I sure did, and Neptune is still cut-up like a Halloween pumpkin as an aftermath, that was an extreme sparring match. I don't know what that's doing to, you know, to gravity, or something, but I haven't noticed anything. Oh, here come a bunch of dragon-stars, most of them having companions, warping down to the field. Damn, they are huge, and Zeus would take a second (or third) seat, look at all those godlike, Shire horse muscles! I'm glad Kukulkan isn't playing, he's a benign, massive clenched saurian mega-fist, his muscles have muscles, that are having muscles-galore. Oh, look, it's Soreidian setting down, too, and I guess this is his 20 Lizardanians, right, John?

MADDENHAWK: You called it accurately, Frank. It's kickoff time, and it's going to be a wild game! After the incredible play by Rachel Dreadnought resulting in a 115-yard score, and the extra point kicked in professionally by Jason Shireman, the condition of the field is, well, a proverbial battlefield. And just look at that! After the touchdown, Rachel turned around to Katrina on the sidelines, licked her thumb, and wiped her own backside, and did a little sneer and whoosh, wow, right at Katrina's gawking face! Back to the field, the surface looks like heavy artillery hit it, like in World War One. The talons on the reptilians depress the ground like gangpunching tank treads, grounding up the artificial turf, a phantasmagoria of dark dirt. I'm afraid it's rocks underneath the dirt, littered all over the field, digging deep. The Black World weapons are clearing the field, but it's sand against a cyclone, really, sand against some epic, tsunami wave. In fact, every play is mega-epic: claws and extreme bites are legion. The dragon-roars are completely devastating and really egg on this crowd. There is nothing to 'hold' on to when the saurians tackle, so they tackle with their teeth, jaws and it's a literal bloodbath out there. On this field, though, it's a cold, muscle-hard game, and that's all there is to it. The 5,000-seat stadium is now full-up and people are wide-eyed at this fantasia-like, throw-down game.

FACENDA: Second and one. Katrina hands off to Korillia in a draw-play. Korillia got five yards, but it took three-quarters of the Black Fins to bring her down. Pandemonium, the field got chewed up again, with this hand-off. This took about three minutes off the clock. I'm amazed that these plays take so long. They almost always result in a touchdown. I haven't seen a punt yet. Now Katrina, play action, lots of time in the pocket, and there is Ettoros, he jumps up (below the five feet he is allowed) and takes the ball away from Danillia in a mid-air wrestling match, touchdown, Green Fins! Oh my God, after the play, Danillia is beating the holy hell out of Ettoros, and that, after the whistle. Danillia is still creaming Ettoros, and wow, snap, snap and snap again! I heard the breaking of bones right here in the broadcasting booth. With a huge roar, Danillia had Ettoros' legs in her mouth, just lifted that thousand-pound-saurian up, and using her inconceivable jaws, thunder clapped and bone-smashed his limbs together. You can see Ettoros' feet and his upper leg have been joined in an ecstasy of awesome-crunch. Unbelievable. Ettoros is on the ground, in incredible pain, and the Green Fins have to take a time out to attend to him. Now, I don't see him moving at all, his bones all mangled around. And still no flags! It's just preposterous that with such an obvious and obnoxious foul, there is no penalization. I guess that's an example of just being 'Lizzie overpowered.' Danillia is saying something, get some sound on her, pronto. And she's laughing too and here it is: "You know what the humans say at a time like this, right Ettoros? Rest in so-many-pieces, saurian scumbag. Hell, I could take reptilian males and make any squeezebox out of you; I'd crush your head in my massive quads like any proverbial Allosaurus."

FACENDA: Green Fins have the ball midway up the field. Second and six, and a hoard of Black Fins were there on first down, remember. Kerok is looking to the sky, and I guess there is a signal to throw. On the previous play, Ettoros received the ball from Katrina, and it was a bullet, then he was tackled by Oriasel, Saleosian, Penemuelian (that particular Lizzie, Penemuelian, is tremendously dominant at over 11 feet tall), and Verrierian. Katrina is back to pass again. She's running all over the field and can't find a Green Fin to pass to! Minutes are being burned off the clock, as everyone is fighting and then fighting someone else. Total mayhem out there. And this method of battle is full throw-down, they are really punching out the ying-yang, and humans would be literally obliterated by those saurian punches. The Black Fins are beating the Green Fins slowly down. Soreidian himself breaks free of Littorian and is running after Katrina too! Soreidian is only a step or two away from the teenager's fragile frame. Kat suddenly throws, deep in the collapsing pocket, yup, it's an incomplete pass. And Rahabian, coaching the Black Fins, is raging at the officials at this point, frightening those swords something awful. And what is this? A late flag on the play. An officiating sword is now making an announcement.

INTENTIONAL GROUNDING, QUARTERBACK, OFFENSE, LOSS OF DOWN, FOURTH DOWN.

Wow, that was a good call, Kat might have been fearing for her life. I would be, with a dinosaur like Soreidian chasing me around the field. There have been other calls that deserved a flag, but the Black World swords aren't throwing any, and I guess we are all used to that. Kat confers with Kerok and the coach is looking to the sky again! The teenager, on a long snap, fades back and, look at that, she's running around, looking for an open receiver! Kat throws a picture-perfect and beautiful spiral. Valacian and Korillia both went up for the ball and, oh my God, Korillia pushed her claws through the throat of Valacian, and makes the incredible catch and it's a touchdown. The dragoness left the lifeless saurian in the end zone, doesn't concern herself at all with him, and she does a Darryl Dawkins on the goal post and brings the whole structure down, it's flattened, demolished. The crowd is going bat-crap-crazy. And, of course, no flags, no ejections, no nothing on the part of the officiating

Black World swords, who, are facing a crumpled goal post. Worried, they are thinking that the post is totally shot, as Korillia massively makes a huge muscle show, doing any miscellaneous Warrior Pose. Katrina is beside herself, congratulating Korillia on an excellent play. Korillia crushed Valacian with so much muscularity, taking the rock right through Valacian's esophagus, and he hasn't moved yet either. Kat is probably figuring that the dragons will take care of the injured Black Fin. Valacian is being removed from the field, Soreidian doing the honors of just lifting the lifeless body up and bringing him over to the Black Fins bench. The Alligatorian and Lizardanian medical crews are running over to see what they can do on Valacian.

FRANK FACENDA: With 20 minutes in a quarter, that's 80 minutes of raw and cruel football, and already, the field is decimated, but not as bad as both teams inflicting such suffering (that is to say, on the field). Teresian will be defending her companion, Katrina at the guard position, right next to Littorian, Teresian came in on an injury. What do you think of the positions, these creatures are muscle-Mack trucks.

MADDENHAWK: That's right, Frank, and the field, this artificial turf must be screaming in pain with this talon-stomping going on, 1,000 pounds of dynamic sinews, and, look, the saurians are going an inch or two into that strained grass, just casually walking along, with their Atlas selves. This field looks like turf, but it's actually made of 20,000 recycled tires, because, like everything in Oregon, go-recycle, right? It cuts down on mowing, that's for sure. That's got to take a toll on the artificial grass, but it's all recyclable, it's true. However, here's my question, can that offensive line give time to Katrina to make a big play? I've never seen any of them in action, so surprises all around tonight. The saurians can only jump up to five feet, and then they will earn a penalty. And the highest throw or kick can be 500 feet up, and no more. Personally, I'm thinking it's going to be bullet passes. The Roman coliseum's traditions are set to meet the mighty saurians here at Peter Stott field tonight, get ready!

FACENDA: There's the snap, and Katrina fakes a hand-off and is going to throw. Her offensive line is handling the Black Fins' onslaught, but barely. Katrina throws to Ettoros, a real bullet, and he's confronted by an enstrengthened pack of Black Fin players, for a nine-yard gain. Looking at the line, it is all mashed up by those saurians, the Black World weapons will be hard-pressed to level the field, now that it's being torn up, the Astroturf, just a fading memory. Even though the whistle has blown, Littorian and Soreidian are really going at it, biting and brawling, there are really fighting! I have word from a Black World sword that a respite has been offered by Soreidian! The answer is obvious. They fight on, despite the whistle. No one is saying anything, seconds are going by, Katrina disregards this isolated carnage, and is huddling with the rest of the Green Fin players. It doesn't matter if Soreidian or Littorian are part of the plan, they have their own bloody scheme. A Black World sword is telling the center and the middle linebacker that the play is over, but they still keep snapping and biting. The sword intervenes between the saurians, many minutes going by (but not on the official clock!) and they go back to their huddles, finally, and Soreidian came off worse. It doesn't really matter because the center and the Middle Linebackers' jobs are quite simple. Wrestle, bite, rip and overall-fighting until the whistle sounds, and I guess, after the whistle, too.

Katrina takes the snap and fades back, in a Run-Pass Option. She throws over the middle in a 72-yard pass to Anakimian, and he puts on the dragon afterburners, and makes a touchdown! He jumped up just under the five-foot rule, catching it with his tail no less, then placed the football in his ripped left arm, and Black Fins couldn't tackle him. Katrina is elated and then some. And still, after the play is over, Littorian and Soreidian are still raging, and there are no flags. The kicking unit is out now, and still, those two are wrestling and they are biting and clawing and now there is blood, and a lot of blood, on both sides. Brian's sword is putting a stop to it, and Soreidian hit the sword, in frustration. Wow, that sword was blown away at that super hit, 30 yards back up the field, landing in a depression! A lot of official Black World swords are sorting things, and the two antagonists back off. The military people are taking notes, only a saurian causes damage to a saurian, or a Black World sword, I guess. I've never seen a reptilian go up against a BWS, that's got to be something new.

GRIFFORD: BWS is Black-World-Sword, right Frank?

FACENDA: You got it, Howie! The time these plays take off the clock is incredible, and that's because the quarterbacks are very fast and smart and with such fantastic defenders. Did you know that the last play took five whole minutes off the game? Incredible and so, so brutal! Look at this insurmountable damage to the field on that one play. These swords are doing a great job leveling it all out with their blades, but it's hopeless. Still, the weapons are trying to get the ground even. The reptilian's talons are doing most of the damage and the tackling is making mighty holes like a dozen howitzers, and that's on every play! The fans are in pleasant shock over the destruction on the battered field.

GRIFFORD: Yeah, and the sparring match continues between Littorian and Soreidian, I couldn't take my eyes off that incredible fight. I'm sorry, but every horse-like muscle on both reptilians was on patent display, it seemed like two sinuous Clydesdales were at war, and there was blood, bone, entrails, and flesh all over the place. You know how many flags have been thrown with that continuous fighting? None! The officiating Black World Swords are turning a blind eye to the carnage. The Lord of the Lizardanians and Soreidian, his deputy, are bleeding, and there is no cure, no magic, no 'getting better' and they will have to last the whole game before they get any treatment, I understand. The other dragons have Alligatorians running around curing injuries, but the swords told me that between the top two, this could be to the death, and no one is stopping it.

FACENDA: Wow…

KINGSTON: Wow.

MADDENHAWK: Wow!

GRIFFORD: Littorian's team will kick off. A Black Fin is preparing to receive. Penemuelian is looking to go end-to-end, 110 yards with this one and he had to bat the ball inbounds, that was a super move, and he tossed it to himself. The reptilians are so, so fast. Look at him go, straight up the middle! The blocking is unbelievable, saurians getting thrown around by the Black Fins team. Thank goodness that the hatchets and knives are reinforcing that tank perimeter, otherwise fans would be dying all over the place. The Green Fin players are bouncing into the tank barrier everywhere, really challenging the hatchets and knives, their black forms are growing white with the energy drain, sheering that power up rather than out. Unbelievable. I can't even understand those vicious blocks; they flattened all the Green Fin defenders. The hang-time of the kick wasn't a factor at all, Brian's kick was right on target. Brian Miller tried a tackle too and got the stiff arm from Penemuelian, sending Brian to the ground too. A human being trying to tackle a dragon? He is very lucky to be getting up, limping to the sidelines. I just can't believe it, it was a professional run, and the NFL better take notice, I've never seen (anywhere) the like. He ran here, there, and everywhere, and that's why his front line could have put Brian Miller in an early grave, too. Thank God he's the only human on the field. And then, after the touch down, Penemuelian dunks the rock through the goal posts, his iron reptilian hands then breaks off the whole structure, Darryl Dawkins all over again! The dismembered post hit one of the tanks and put a hole through it. The knives and hatchets barely held on to that unbelievable saurian force applied, generating it up and not out. Penemuelian took a victory lap around the whole field. After his lap, the goal post is repaired by the attentive swords. The officials did give Penemuelian everything but the bird, but as an anarchist, he didn't care in the least. Penemuelian is given no warning by the officiating swords, either. They just looked the other way. "Let the dragons be dragons" that's the watch-word of the officiating Black World swords, I guess. What do you think of that, John Maddenhawk, you think magic was involved?

MADDENHAWK: The only folks that can use magic here are the BWWs, Howard, everyone else, yellow-flag-penalized.

GRIFFORD: That's Black World Weapons, right?

MADDENHAWK: That's right, Howie!

GRIFFORD: Let's get back to the action. It's a high, floating kick from the Black Fins team, and it's out of the end zone, and glancing off the goal post, rocking the thing like a mizenmast in a giant storm. Luckily, it's a clear and hot night tonight! First down on the 20, Katrina at quarterback. We are nearing the end of the first quarter and look at all the injuries on these saurians! I've never seen so much blood and gore. I guess we know what multiple sparring matches are like, because even after the whistle, these brawls continue for a few seconds, and there will be blood, gallons of it. The lineup must be frightening to Katrina, but she seems at ease. I notice that there are Alligatorians on Soreidian's side of the field, helping with injuries. Super-caked-blown dirt everywhere, increasingly looking more and more like World War One! The further this game goes, the angrier, and the more frustrated the saurians become, and that's probably due to these sparring matches. Katrina hands off to Korillia and there is nothing doing, as Oriasel, Saleosian, Azzaian, and Buneian all combine on Korillia, and she loses 19 yards, and the reason was, she wouldn't go down. When Littorian released Soreidian with his seven-inch teeth, he piled on Korillia, too. All those Black Fins leveled her down to the ground. She was carrying 5,000 pounds with all those saurians tackling her, but that's nothing to this Warlord of Lizardania. Unbelievably, this play took an incredible two minutes off the clock. Katrina, second down and a mile, 29 yards to be exact. She is fading back, in her own end zone, fading right, fading left, she has all day. No one is open so she just threw it away and a lucky fan caught the ball. And got thrown back to the people behind him, too. Luckily it wasn't thrown that hard. Third down. Meanwhile, Katrina's companion is taking out Black Fin Lizardanians left and right, she's a Wysterian, the strength, the power is turning the BWWs white-hot with the energy they are lifting out of the stadium, and the Moon might be a factor, because I'm seeing it now, and it's nearly full. Teresian came in when the Green Fins had an injury. Now Kerok is having some words on the sidelines with Tiperia and Joan of Arc, maybe anticipating something down the road. I don't know what that's about. Kerok is looking pretty grave. I can tell because the 'smile' they always sport is looking like an un-smile right now. I don't know if this is just some playful foreshadowing, but I sure hope it will last.

KINGSTON: I'm just talking to the officiating swords, and they see the problem with the Moon. They are adjusting the energy and power fields, so I guess they'll take care of it. There is a lot of science and math involved, better left to bigger sword brains, right? Counts me out. Howard?

GRIFFORD: Thanks, Maddy. Third down for Katrina, in the shotgun, at her own two-yard line. She is almost out of bounds in her own end zone. Now she's running around, all day and then some, her offensive line going down slowly, saurians robustiously going after each other, no flags, so far. Katrina, oh, she throws a bullet pass, 92 yards, Clareina is there, makes the catch, and then she bulls over Azzaian, Valacian and Verrierian and it's a touchdown! Three minutes passed when Clareina was fighting to get into the end zone, and I've never seen a workhorse doubling as a saurian woman, what a muscle-packed, Cyclopean, pulsing, female ultra-stallion she (sure) is. It was the epitome of epic-city. Damn, she's good, wow, Clareina is laying down and doing a Cobra Pose, just look at that indescribable, totally ripped chest and all those gorgeous, puissant abdominals, a total of twelve of those devastating, city-destroying, pouting structures. And that incredible, swooping tail, that's kinda sexy there, if the audience can forgive me for saying so. I know the pose because my wife practices Yoga, and it's extra-special on a serpent, geez; what do you think, John, and look at that blood-coated field and all these scores, too?

CHAPTER TWO

QUARTER TWO

JOHN MADDENHAWK: IT'S AMAZING TO SEE THEM accomplishing these touchdowns. Yes, that Cobra Pose made me, uh, uncomfortable and excited, I felt awkward and extremely thrilled at the same time. Yes, all the blood, it's totally unheard of (of course)!

HOWARD GRIFFORD: Epicosity supreme, John! Now it's first and 10 at the 20 in the second quarter. NFL-wise the rock would be placed at the 25-yard line, but the officiating swords think the 20 is good enough. I can't believe the performance by Rachel and Katrina during this game...and the score is tied again. It's a draw play, orchestrated by the talented Rachel, and by Uzzaious and he's headed for the right sidelines with incredible speed. Now he's headed back the other way! The defenders stay with him, he's staying on the perimeter, now he's turned around, then the other, looking for that break, and the minutes are ticking off the clock, and Uzzaious is still running. Oh, my God, he's decided to pass, and he has that option, and it's a real bullet, touchdown to Danillia, and that rock was thrown at 253 miles an hour at least, and caught but Danillia, just amazing. That measurement was made by our Unmanned Aerial

Vehicle, which the officiating swords have allowed. Incredible, and they add the extra point, so it's now 56 to Soreidian's 63. And that's half-time, and the injuries are extreme and unbelievable, and I've a report from Maddy that three saurians have lost their lives. The amazing medical team from the Alligatorians and the Lizardanians are trying to bring back the wrecked saurian bodies. The carnage is incredible, and I think they will need some more gurneys on the sidelines. Littorian and Soreidian aren't getting any treatment at all, sitting down in Sphinx style, bleeding, two prize fighters going at it strong. Is that hate in their eyes, or what, Maddy?

KINGSTON: It's not hate, I think Soreidian is respecting Littorian very greatly right about now. It's pretty complicated, but I'm just guessing, here. He's hitting Littorian with all the power he has in his whole body, and yet, Littorian hasn't lost that smile. The thing is, people are of the opinion that dragons are always smiling, but on certain occasions, like sparring matches, you can see them frowning.

CHAPTER THREE
QUARTER THREE

FRANK FACENDA: IT LOOKS LIKE THE ENTIRE FIELD IS A THROW-back to World War One, Verdun or the Somme, and if you need to see that on youtube.com, then go ahead! The ground itself looks like howitzers and heavy railway guns pounded everything. Visual viscera the end result. It's a timber yard of a giant-saw-Earth-mill. The physicality and raw power of the reptilians is indescribable, and if it wasn't for the Black World weapons directing the energy up into the air and not sideways, the incredible force would crush the surrounding buildings and the humans would be bloodily compressed by the shockwaves. I think the fans owe their very lives to the weapons, and don't even know it. The great swords have leveled out the ground, with their blades, but it's so close to hopeless.

FACENDA: The Green Fins got a touchdown, now the Black Fins have the ball. Katrina and Rachel are taking turns, racking up the touchdowns. And these two quarterbacks are having the most vicious conversations, and I'm not going to say what is said, but it is ghetto-bad, believe me. And it goes back and forth, back and forth, Green, Black, Green, Black, touchdown, touchdown, touchdown.

The quarterbacks are amazing and can easily throw the ball way over 100 yards at incredible speeds. They look one way, and throw the other, a technical point, but a good way to avoid an interception.

JOHN MADDENHAWK: The slowness of the reptilians is so overrated, totally. It's just like watching a tennis match, back and forth, and the reptilians are the oversized tennis balls. Both quarterbacks have well over 700 yards during this game. You'd think Katrina and Rachel would be tired, but they aren't. Let me just add in something that will doubtless be edited out, but this is the conversation taking place between these two quarterbacks, thanks to my voice team, good job, guys, and damn, it's rough, and thanks to a certain Black Sword for translating it for us:

You don't know who you are fucking with, right Kat skank, I will fuck your cellulite, wad-ass the hell up, stupid ho!

I'll hammer you right down your American throat, you irregular, gawking, fawking Soreidian whore, even my grandmother could be a faster quarterback!

Lay her out on this field, my saurian gods, Kat doesn't deserve your mercy, kick her silly, bastardized-back-side!

This nasty, fat, fille de joie, *let me piss on her ashes, just where in the home-cooking-southern-fuck do you get your crap from, dog-shitting-scoliosis-looking-bitch?*

I need her flabby head ripped off so I can shit down it forever-and-a-day; any saurian that gets me that crown, I'll, I'll, I'll give you the time of your vast amount of lives!

If you play dirty as fuck, I'll do the same thing, I'm not scared of you goddamn, libertine, slime-ball, tramp!

Wow, that's (surely) enough!

CHAPTER FOUR

QUARTER FINALE

GRIFFORD: The score is moving up fast, 105 to 112, 112 to 119, 119 to 126, 126 to 128. Every time, it's more than likely a touchdown resulting from each possession, taking minutes off the clock, as each quarterback goes running around the field, looking for an open receiver. Now it's 132 to 140, and I don't know how we got here, either! The extra point was just missed too, that's what we have letting teenager males play the game of football, I guess. We are ending the 4ᵗʰ quarter and the two-minute mark, and, oh no! The blitz got by and Katrina got her wrist and arm broken, yes, both. Cameras akimbo, we can see Kat's injury. The wounds make you shutter at home. What do you think of that, John?

MADDENHAWK: It's very serious and Danillia is the center of interest in this event. Magic is what can cure Katrina, Teresian is trying this now, but the magic is being stopped by Danillia! The Wysterian is looking forlorn at this brand of magic and is watching Danillia breaking Kat's arm on her own sidelines symbolically, just like cracking a stick, but it's for real, and the arm is snapped again! Danillia is smiling broadly. The pain must be incredible.

Wow, Teresian, the Wysterian, is really blowing up on the sideline, pointing to Danillia. Geez, the entire field experienced an 11 or 12 Richter scale earthquake as a magical dinosaur is conjured up by Teresian. It's a Tyrannosaurs Rex running at Danillia! Now a colossal magical Griffin is being coaxed from Danillia, with a titanic set of rippling, muscled wings. They are wrestling it out on mid-field. The crowd is going crazy, egging the magical candescences on! The supernatural dinosaur is definitely winning, but it was Joan of Arc that intervened yet again, bringing this magic ride to a sudden armistice. No one wants to hurt Joan of Arc, even the paranormal creatures held sway, just waiting for word to war again. Amid the horrible blood and lizard-torn-carnage, Joan of Arc is taking the field for the final two minutes for Littorian's team! This is Joan of Arc and everyone is listening to her. She'll be the quarterback because of the magical breaking of Katrina's right arm. There are multiple flags on the play, because magic is being used, not allowed. I can hear Two Steps from Hell as she makes her way to the huddle. Two minutes and the Green Fins are down eight points, obviously she will have to go for the two-point conversion. The fight between Littorian and Soreidian might hang in the balance and does she have the time to make it down a huge wall of saurian muscle to the goal line and that, twice? After all, at the conclusion of the game, the two saurian leaders will have a sparring match, and only one will survive. The only thing she has is to get the receiver out of bounds to stop the clock. She's in the shotgun and obviously Joan is going to throw, just like any writer, throwing for the end zone (of course!). The speed at which these saurians can move is unbelievable, so Joan will have to throw faster lest she get intercepted. I feel sorry for the fans, this is more like a tennis match than a typical football game. Maddy, Katrina is injured, can you see her down on the field?

KINGSTON: I can, I can, Katrina, you have a broken arm, can't a magic spell fix you right back up again?

CHAKIAYA: Hi, Maddy, and it's a Danillia spell, alright, and she's keeping me from playing these last two minutes. I'm thinking of words to describe that female saurian but I'm afraid the fans will just have to speculate on what those are.

KINGSTON: So, I guess this is frustration to your companion, right here with us, and it's going to draw a flag on the play, right, isn't that right, Teresia?

TERESIAN: You bet it is, and I'm not afraid to describe that sorcerous bitch breaking my companions' arm over and over when I've got it healed. She's a big, fat—

CHAKIAYA: Yeah, I'll have to interrupt my companion now, and I won't do that normally, but, my gracious queen, we are on the cusp of a compromise, right? My second, Joan of Arc, is going to take over, now, where is she?

KINGSTON: If Joan takes command of the field, with two minutes to go, I'll have to interview her again. And what is this? Wow, Katrina is singing, yes, singing the Russian National Anthem! Standing there with a broken arm, tears on her proud face, singing. And now, all the Black World weapons are chiming in, too, providing some fantastic orchestration, it sounds great, like the St. Petersburg Children's choir brought to the Peter W. Stott Community Field. All the companions on the Green Fin side have joined in the singing, maybe Katrina is giving the words of the song in her dragon-inspired telepathy! The Black Fin companions are silent, though, but respectful. Every saurian is just gaping at the high-shrilled human singing, unbelievable. Oh, here is The Maid of Orleans!

JOAN OF ARC: Yes, I liked Katrina's Russian anthem, it was great. It inspired me, too. Facing the front, I have all day to get a score here, and two-points too, I know the rules, Christ help my anarchist saurians to see those so-called 'guidelines' in this civil society, oh!

KINGSTON: Yup, it seems you're taking over. This was the second time you've had to, right? The last time was the French army, bringing it to victory. The thing about taking Paris we can just set aside. How do you feel about taking over as quarterback, Joan?

JOAN OF ARC: I will play for Katrina. Hey, Danillia, I'm for you! Please allow Katrina to heal! I'm her back-up and it was my idea anyway. You want a human life to mess up? Then take me! That's enough interviewing let me go to work, God bless me, Maddy.

KINGSTON: Wow, Danillia is responding, can we pick that up, too, let's get some sound on her reply!

DANILLIA: You'll use Lizardanians and Alligatorians as doctors for those killed on this field? With you humans here, this good work is good for nothing. Like all work on this miserable planet. They should put toe-tags on you in anticipation of our 11 saurians killing you to death, Joan of Arc, and over death, sending your ashes into any Black Hole, I'll 86 you myself! I dispute your 'talking to God,' and you are a witch and a heretic, and I'll have you unmercifully end in my strengthened teeth! You'll see me in corded muscle-form that will put everyone into the deepest shadows, to give my battle again. You still wanna take this field? I'll chew-and-cud-mash-you-three-times-to-death-and-over!

JOAN OF ARC: Oh, I've seen better film on baby fangs, Danillia. And I place myself between Katrina and the pressed-down-horrible-darkness of this magic spell, and by Holy Christ, too! If you're on a sincere mission, that's permission. I will have you out on that field, face me like any woman will. I will not tolerate your weaponizing my sublime feelings. Release your spell on Kat, God be praised!

KINGSTON: Wow, what an exchange between Danillia and Joan of Arc. And Danillia (and Teresian) have complied, the spells and magic are gone. Joan of Arc will be quarterbacking for these last two minutes, it's 132 to 140, hold on to what's left of your butts, fans!

CHAPTER FIVE

TWO MINUTE WARNING

GRIFFORD: FALSE STARTS, OFFSIDES, PEAL-BACK BLOCKS, HEAD-butting, tripping, holding, none of that has been called during this entire game. Joan must have God himself directing her, there are no errant throws by that quarterback. Anakimian wants to play another position but Joan says no, keep playing wide receiver. Then she winks at him! Plainly, Anakimian is afraid of what Danillia will do, if there is a blitz. Danillia will feast on Joan like any massive great white shark going after a guppy. She's got two minutes, and she has to use it all, because the Black Fins will almost certainly get a touchdown, with any time left. Here's the snap! Joan is handing it off, and after a 10-yard run, Korillia gets out of bounds. Korillia was so bit, mauled and blasted physically by the Black Fins team, but, of course, no flags. Korillia brushed herself off, and actually waived to us in the booth, wow! First and 10 again, one minute, forty-two seconds. Joan fades back, now up in the pocket, she's going to the right, and she throws a speeder to Anakimian, and he is absolutely drilled, like down in a crater, and they are at mid-field. The officiating Black World Swords level the ground with their blades. That is, level for this play, next time, it looks like the Somme. Joan of Arc again, seconds draining from the clock, Littorian and Soreidian in a mad-tackling-furious fight at the line of scrimmage, Joan, looking, looking, throws…and it's complete at the 20-yard line to Anakimian, appropriately and strangely enough, he's out of bounds, stopping the clock. Joan runs over to talk to Kerok about strategy. They have one time-out left. Joan, snapped, play-action pass. Danillia and everyone else, chasing Joan around the field. The blocking is so violent. They always have an overloaded front, but it's teeth, claws, talons, everything is employed by the offensive line, blood, flesh, I've even seen a leg and an arm blown off by the defense, the power is so much that even a saurian can't fend it off. And the tail-whipping! That illegal move is used on both sides, and it is deviation-writ-large, and it is concentrated on saurians, so far. But a tail-whip could take a human's head to the sky. If the Green Fins score here and there is no time left, they can still go for the extra point, according to the Black World swords officiating this contest. Littorian's team, down by eight points. They are going to rush only two Black Fins, this time. It's all kinds of pressure on Joan, but she doesn't show it. It's a time out on the field now. Look at all that long blond hair sported by Joan, Maddy what do you think?

KINGSTON: It used to be short, now it's luxurious, and streams down almost to the field. I think it's lovely hair, Howie, and I hope it isn't, you know, pulled out raw by this strong Soreidian defense. I guess the time is now! The Green Fins wish to go for the two-point conversion. Oh, what is this, Tiperia is suited up and is relieving Ettoros playing wide receiver. She lines up at the far end on the left. She already spoke to Joan, and Joan did a double take. She couldn't believe what Tiperia said. Danillia and Soreidian are talking, too. Danillia is worried about Soreidian's condition. He looks like he's been through a meat-saurian-grinder. Littorian looks bad, too, but at least he's smiling. Joan is fading back, looking to the left. Oh my God, Joan is looking to the right, and sails over the blitz by the Black Fins' Azzaian, Uzzaious and Buneian in a ballet-grand jete,

180 degrees, unbelievable, and they tackled nothing, Joan rising like a bird, and saurians ended up in a huge, reptilian heap on the decimated ground! Boy are they pissed off! They even tried a united tail-whip on Joan, as she faked a naked bootleg, and The Maid eluded all those tails, like Keanu Reeves dodging bullets in the Matrix. Jeannette throws a bullet, still airborne, into the welcome arms of Tiperia, Danillia is right there, Tiperia has her two steps in the end zone, and is pounded to the ground, touchdown! It's 138 to 140. Three seconds to go, Green Fins go for the two-point conversion. Joan throws the rock at superspeed and Tiperia makes the catch yet again, it's a tie game! Inconceivable! How could Tiperia, lined up on the left side of the field, appear at the right side all in a second or two? I'm told by the omnipresent Black World officiating swords that Tiperia ran around the _whole world_, in just a second, and then makes the two-point play on a reception from Joan, on the opposite end of the end-zone! I also understand from my aside to the officiating sword, that Tiperia ran over a lake and actually winked at a guy fishing. She got several fishes in the boat itself, with the wake she created, too! Totally unbelievable. Every one of the Black Fins jump on Tiperia, trying to cause a fumble. Except for Soreidian. He's just down on the ground with Littorian standing over him. Danillia, gave the round-the-world tight end a real going over, too. I'm not sure if going around the world is a good play, but there are no flags thrown, so I guess it was okay to do! Littorian is walking over to Tiperia. Danillia is looking guilty, and the game is tied! Whoops, I think that's it for us commentators, because the Black World weapons are getting us back home! What, you're offering me more money? Sure, I'll take it! Good night, and what a football game! Hey, my Black World swords, doesn't a tie end up leading to overti—

NARRATIVE TAKEN OVER BY BRIAN MILLER:

Abruptly and ridiculously, the commentators were whisked away by the weapons. Just in time, too, overtime rules just won't do.

Littorian left Soreidian, huffing and puffing on the ground. He didn't have the heart to finish him off, and I definitely encouraged him not to take Soreidian's life. The might that Soreidian produced was great, but that couldn't best The Lord of the Lizardanians. Littorian was the superior reptilian. Danillia, also flat on the field, completely exhausted. The remains of Tiperia (loosely put), in a newly-made ditch.

—Are you done with that human being, Danillia? Come on, speak up, peas and carrots in a vermin pod, you want another go?

Danillia said nothing and, like a snake, sulked away. Littorian just dismissed this with a dragon harrumph. He approached Tiperia, all dragon-crushed-and-cracked in a meaningful end-zone crater. The charnel remnants of Tiperia were littered all over the blood-soaked ditch, all entrails and viscera, and innards everywhere-and-otherwise, scattered about. All that malice, the meaningful and clear-eyed intent to hurt, came out of Danillia, beating on Tiperia. She hit her so hard, her bone crushing, organ piledriving and pulverizing, turning Tiperia's viscera into mushy pulp, devastating, kith-and-kin-ripping claws, Danillia had the power to dent the whole Earth in by her mega-pounding. Even though no resistance was offered by Tiperia, those monstrous muscular arms had no mercy in dealing with Tiperia but good. Now, Danillia was utterly drained, not from this Tiperia-pummeling, but the grinding football game overall.

She lowered her head to Littorian, as he walked by her.

—Oh, I thought those silly saurians really finished you off. I'm sure you're not hurt, I mean, other than being all scattered around. Can you pull yourself together for me? My epitome question: How do you feel?

Littorian held out a hand.

And then everything flowed back into the stunning picture of a human woman again!

I was worried about Tiperia, at first. She was so hideous after that joint-saurian beating, I looked away. Then, of a sudden, she looked like she's never been utterly destroyed at all. She took Littorian's hand, rose up. Littorian, amused, spoke again.

—Ah, like the Phoenix, is that random enough for you?

—I feel great. Danillia couldn't stop my love for you, Littorian. Never mind about that. You won't fight Soreidian, right?

—I already have. The football game took it all out of Soreidian, his anger is dissipated. I did this for you and Brian, not killing Soreidian. Now Soreidian owes Brian again, insurance for him, down the road, I guess. We are all but ready to leave Earth. Oh, maybe you could terraform Mars for the humans, just as a nod to Brian, perhaps? That'd give the humans something to do, they like building rockets (to the stars)!

CHAPTER SIX

JEANNETTE ASCENDING

I ARRIVED AT JOAN OF ARC'S MINI-MINI CASTLE AT OUR CAMP IN THE Everglades. Soon enough, the outpost would go to human hands. The castle was attached on the main house by a quaint, little drawbridge. The totally enterprising Black World weapons had constructed it all for Joan, out of French mortar and bricks making it look like a castle from the 1400s. Anything to make Joan feel more at home.

I opened the medieval door (cleverly Black World weapon-designed) and, refreshingly, light music was playing. It was time to draft another leader, a better leader to the 30 Companions. I was really looking forward to it, I'd speak to Jeanette directly.

And Joan was dancing around, and, damn, I thought she was raving drunk as a lady-lord! Her hair was a massive-blond-genius, tingling-down-and-richly-down, almost to the marble floor. She was singing along with Karen Carpenter and the song was "Close To You," and she was prancing around with flower petals galore, sprinkled everywhere and anyhow:

...just like me,
they long to be,
close to you!

I thought about Karen's life, feeling that Jeannette had no idea. That was good, I didn't feel like being a cloud over Joan of Arc, dragging her down. I gently closed the door, saving the surrender of the 30 companions for another time, and face to face with Korillia! I swallowed asphalt, forcing my smile.

—Oh, glad to see you, my lady. You did a great job as Running Back during the game. I know your intention is to see Jeannette, but this global warming thing has me really concerned, and I think the Wysterian could use your help and I also think—

As usual, she just blew me off, with the trivial hand gesture, making those seven-inch claws come uncomfortably close to my face. I didn't back up, so assured was I with her grace. Naturally, I trusted her completely.

—Ah, not to worry my silly Terran, Teresian has that on her list, forget this 'warming' stuff and concentrate on leaving this whore Earth or I will take you away myself. This is just a product of your shitty environment, what else is new? Clareina and Larascena will thank me for taking you away from Earth. Are you blocking that door, so I can't get to Joan? This, like all human stuff, has gone on too long. As you know, the end of this new beginning is near. How do you feel?

—In your presence, my lady, I feel fine. It's only been a few months, how does that compare to someone who has lived eons, like you? Like people down South say, "Let the slick end slide and the rough end drag," right? Please, just look at this rough-and-miscellaneous grocery bag, oh, it's alright if you take it, I know you're a dragon-star and would take it anyway. It's just a for-instance, speaking of global warming, a bag you'd get at the supermarket. First, as you see, it's light brown paper, not plastic, so it's not like contributing to the plastic-lakes in the oceans. I understand the

Black World Swords are doing something about that as a favor for the 30 companions, and that's great. Look at this, the bag has got the weight, in pounds, that it can hold, well, six pounds! And it's got the makers of the bag on the side of it, three people made this bag, see their names? And it was made in the USA, you see, giving jobs to those people, and perhaps more. It's got a serial number on it, and the renewable, recyclable and sustainable stuff on there, too. I know I'm being quite forward with you now, Korillia. I think Global Warming is a real concern and I'm bold enough to talk about whatever it is, even without substantial information or the facts. The scientists got it figured out, so I look to them. It contains a minimum (hear that, a minimum!) of 40% post-consumer material already! It's almost recyclable now, what do you think, my lady and heir apparent Warlord of Lizardania, Korillia?

Korillia's permanent smile went down as I concluded my little speech. That's hard to do, if your born a star dragon. I needed her to smile more, not less. She took the bag from my generous hand, faking a smile. Of a sudden, she punched through the bag, with her mighty fist (no big deal there) but then the reptilian crushed up the bag and put her condensed fist, inches from my face, and really crunched it down, vibrating slightly. The Lizardanian crushed the paper to miniature-nothing, with a fist that could level any mountain, her 50-plus-inch biceps erupting, pouting and pulsing. Korillia revealed her sleek, scaled palm, and there with just the very slightest dust, which she proceeded to blow in my astounded mug.

—There. Now I've cured this global warming myself, with your little bag. Yes, scientist know a lot, right, like bleeding people, and taking cadavers and drinking their blood, and now you believe in what they are telling you today, or yesterday?

Strangely, even with this miniscule-power display, I felt more comfortable with being with the saurians every day, such feats of strength notwithstanding. Maybe this was just the "emerging dragon" in me, just trying to be at home, change is life's nature and it's hope.

—What other favors have you got, my little human nizzle?

—I think getting out of this conversation is my best course, my lady.

Korillia departed with a little dragon-esque flourish, darting her city-and-county-smashing fingers around, benignly of course.

—It seems so, concern yourself with our leaving procedures so we can finally get going, I was just about to tell Joan of Arc myself! However, I guess Tiperia and Joan of Arc have the floor right now, right?

CHAPTER SEVEN

AFTERMATH-IMAGEMAKER

AFTER THE VERY EPIC FOOTBALL GAME, JEANETTE MANAGED THAT very fatal predilection given to some teenagers: Thinking. She could see the whole world, the one in the 1400s and today. How little mankind had advanced, how very little, so few noble and fallacious thoughts were present now-days. This was not 'new' (and nothing is, under the sun) but the very concept of 'companionship' <u>in this sense</u> (and I say that with real emphasis) was something modern. That's what Joan thought about, another race 'got something' out of companionship, needed the advice of humanity, young advice.

Of Tiperia, that Starfinder considered the general plan, in retrospect.

The actions on that football field were designed to wear-out the saurians in a passionate game. All this was orchestrated by Tiperia. She loved Littorian, knowing the situation very well. The secret was Joan. Tiperia knew of Soreidian's might, something so powerful, humans could be swept up and *kaput*-ted. Human beings could be so intricate, so profound, and could love-so-endlessly. The Starfinder also knew that love was strong, but love didn't have any antitank guns, grenades, mortars, nuclear weapons, airplanes, and all those war-weapons that was the *real-politick* of modern times. She wanted to preserve the companion program, the teenagers guiding the anarchist saurians, but how to keep Soreidian and Littorian from killing each other over it all? Joan of Arc offered her a way out. Jeannette had some crazy religious ways. Tiperia respected those ideas, too. Thesis, Antithesis and eventually Synthesis, good building blocks to infuse in Joan. Then, learning that, she would see how you have to <u>change</u> your ideas given time. And that time-infinity Tiperia did have. Even 'truth' could be measured given time, and human understanding must reach a 'new' Synthesis, change is constant, you had to be flexible in your thinking. Remember, even here, power can 'create' truth (but can it maintain it, forever?). Truth is limited, that's the indictment of truth. So non-power can create non-truth in the minds of the people. People are like fish, all grouped together, lemmings to the world and if everyone declares it to be truth, then that's the way. Only later do you see what fools humanity always is, and probably, was. Saying there is no 'later' doesn't make it so. There is a 'later,' the double-indictment of mankind.

Tiperia had one weakness, however: She loved Littorian. He was so infinitely strong, he could love her, her way, and far, far over it. So Littorian must be preserved. Soreidian was a Lizardanian, and hated Brian Miller. The Starfinder applied her secret hope: Joan of Arc.

CHAPTER EIGHT

REWARDED—SORT OF

Happy it was all over and happier too that the leading saurians were completely exhausted, Joan of Arc had a victory celebration with Tiperia—sort of. The god was pleased, Joan had saved Tiperia's lover.

—Anything you want, Jeanne la Pucelle, you ask, and I will bend Space, Time and Distance, my episodic and nemesis Trinity and it's all yours, come, what do you need from me? The fact that you and Dracula have a year together, well, I conclude that's just coincidence. Coincidences do exist, but they are rare, still, I'm of the opinion that they happen. However, thesis, antithesis and synthesis, right? It's just a pack of little white lies (that is thesis and antithesis fighting it out) building up to our 'bigger' synthesis, the bigger justified truth. For now, that's the truth. Later, it will become a lie, too, after it breaks down with thesis and antithesis, okay? I claim the right to _change my mind_, as any good woman should. That is the universal Right of Woman, to change her mind. So, again, your desires?

—I'm sure your aware of my yearning to rescue the Donner Party. Let me take a temporary rain check on my wish, perhaps I will need it later on. I'd like to guide my own companion, my lady, and that's all you can do for me. If the Donner Party comes, it comes! If it turns out to be their time, it's their time.

CHAPTER NINE

OUR SOLAR SYSTEM'S (NEW) NINTH PLANET

TERESIAN, THE WYSTERIAN, HER BROTHER KUKULKAN, TOGETHER with a revitalized Littorian and I had a talk about the favors granted to the humans by the dragons. Thing was, 30 'favors' for 30 companions. I didn't even argue with these three dragon-stars about their 'dissipation' of the favors, and everyone just lost track of them anyway. Of course! They are anarchists, and 'saying' their where 30 favors didn't influence them one way or the other. In addition, wildfires were a thing of the past, too, with Crocodilians on-call. They were very skilled at setting up conflagrations outside of fire-starters, burning them out that way. This was considered a pleasantry on the diplomatic side, but in secret, the Crocodilians loved fire.

In addition, Teresian put the Black World weapons on the idea of 'curing the common cold,' as one of the favors for the 30 companions. The Wysterians both felt grieved over the death of the original 30 companions during the harsh reign of Genotdelian, the late Lord of the Crocodilians, as did his successor, Turinian.

In one humorous exchange, they believed that 60 favors should be granted to humanity, with another 30 piled on as an apology for even communicating at all with humans. Those 30 killed companions had family members, and shouldn't they be 'granted' favors? Counting, say, four family members apiece, shouldn't they receive 120 favors? Giving the humans something, they want everything. What about great grandparents, uncles, aunts, half-brothers, half-sisters, and all of that mankind-action? When this conversation got up to the thousands of favors, I knew it was time to bring it to a polite end. Cures to coronavirus, various forms of influenza (and everything so derived in the Spanish flu of 1918), kidney problems, smallpox, Ebola virus, rabies, AIDS-HIV, Hantavirus, Cocoliztli, Dengue, Rotavirus, SARS, MERS, diphtheria, all kinds of plagues, they just took the whole medical book and made antivirals and cures for everything and 'gave it all' to the medical community, closing the world-wide human medical book with a Black-World harrumph. The weapons really wanted a challenge. Look at the human DNA and the juvenile replicating of RNA, had the weapons looking skyward saying "That's all you've got, bitch?". The battle was over in a day and a half. Going further down the list, all the sexual diseases in the nasty, sordid human repertoire were countenanced, too. And after that, 'dealing with' Skid Row and the worst cities in the world without bloodshed, was on tap. That was if (and only if) the dragons could stay around. Afterall, the Black World weapons needed something to do.

What the medical community did with these cures was another affair. Some thought all the viruses were acts of the military, for keeping people in line. The Black World weapons all agreed with the saurian design for leaving humans to figure out humans, they were for departing soon, and with their companions.

—That's your first 'favor,' Brian? Talk about wishing for air to breathe, frickin' wow. You'd better come to me about your priorities in the future.

Lara was watching a movie as a 'last call on Earth' in my office, so I interrupted her.

—Whatja watching, Lara?

—It's _The Lair of the White Worm_, by Bram Stroker, but I'm guessing it's a comedy. You know I don't believe in religion, or the Masons, Illuminati, Scientology, Est, and everything and anything human at all, it's all just associations and contacts, all of it. You humans can't be alone, hence religion. However, I do believe in you, Brian. As to the movie, the fangs are cool. Strange that the bad guys don't have the ultra-strength of real serpents, too bad. Come and watch, find a spot next to me, yes, right there, good, it's a funny movie, enjoy it with me.

—Sure, I will. Say, I was interested in going to Iran with Littorian, just for a visit before we all leave. Can you and Clare accompany us?

—Yeah, sure, I'll go. I'm just following the white dragon on your arm; just watch this movie and let your hands be very liberal! Next I'm going to watch _King Kong vs. Godzilla_, the humans filmed this in 1962, should be fun!

—My lady let's skip out on that one. Besides, you might not like how that one turns out. Now then, let my liberalities begin!

CHAPTER TEN
A Dragon-Star's Afterword by Terminus

Don't interrupt me Brian Miller, again, all saurian previous warnings apply hereafter, hear? I know what was draconianly decided in the other books, beware. I'm watching you, and I've heard about your hidden shenanigans.

I was very grateful I didn't have to defend Sheeta Miyazaki on the football field. I'd have killed Danillia for breaking my companion's arm. I've such an attraction to Sheeta Miyazaki, and I'm not ashamed to say it. The humans who were in the game are lucky not to have been blown to pieces by saurian might. The Black World weapons were watching out for them.

When Brian Miller did meet J. Michael Brower again, that prosaic, error-ridden-scribbler, the author looked more beat-up (not 'upbeat') than before. I laughed, thinking this is what human society does when it's balancing on a scale of complete, total bullshit, it's got our belletrist washed up on a beach like any bloated whale, with a dozen wine bottles littered around him, no less. What an indictment of human-kind; and, of 'indictments,' they are legion.

J. Michael Brower

—You want to see that writer, J. Michael Brower, what—again!? Leave him. You see, he's a 'dying letter' and not a 'novel' novelty.

Brian politely ignored me, has usual. I looked in on them in Brian's once-again repaired office. I lost count on how many times it was destroyed by saurian muscle. I noticed some human emails were scattered about, probably from Michael's valise. These amused me, and I read this (probably unread) email:

David Brown   March 31, 2017
13861 Sunrise Valley Dr. #300
Herndon, VA 20171

J. Michael Brower
5424 SE Gladstone Street
Portland, OR 97206

Dear Mr. Brown!

It's impossible for 'mere' words to describe my state of poverty, at the moment. I work at night as a custodian dealing with my 'disability veteran' status. I really am the least, last and the left out of Trump's revolutionary screed.

It was about 17 years ago when I was a Revolutionary (and no one would touch me) either the Right or the Left. Back then, I was styling myself someone opposed to outsourcing and privatization–while maintaining my 'capitalist' veneer. Long since retired, suffering a major, debilitating stroke, forcing me out, the 'little blip' of 'J. Michael Brower' isn't present in the pages of (benighted) history, I'm jes' a little footnote today. I'm enclosing my support of your enterprise, Network Solutions, herewith. You can still find this article on the web, "U.S. Government Must Maintain Control of Internet" with any search engine. With the Trump 'revolution' a la Stephen K. Bannon (who is himself a perverted "Leninist") I see things that are 'similar' to my view, but I think he's a 'mixed (up) bag'–I don't know your political ideas, but I'm pretty sure they are good ones. Like Ann Coulter said in a video of Trump, "he's a cad." I'm kinda too old to work for a 'cad,' so I'll stay a retired civil servant (when I had a stroke, I was a Captain in the OR Guard).

I've two websites, supported by Network Solutions, www.jmbrower.com and www.stardragons.org. I'm trying to become a writer, but, with "Revolution" cited above, it's just a parody of "Start the Revolution Without Me" now. I don't know your 'relation' to web.com or their 'relation' to you...but I've always the Internet, which brings me back to writing about your company. I wish you can help me out, maybe alleviate this $144 a month I'm paying to web.com? That would be great and would definitely help my 'company.' Thank you for your time! You know, (un)ironically, my 'character' Brian Miller, lives in Herndon, VA, too, and he's a real person. I tried to get your folks to do the following or allow me to get the .html so I could do it myself–in vain. I'm writing you out of desperation. Also, the money involved ($144 a month) I can't afford for much longer. Can you do something for me? Can you get my 'inputs' corrected, sir? Thank you for your ideas.

Yours Warmly!
J. Michael Brower

...and this little human silliness here, unbelievable really; how humans can embarrass themselves is a mystery to saurians, everywhere...

David Brown   May 22, 2017
CEO, the Web Company
13861 Sunrise Valley Dr. #300
Herndon, VA 20171

J. Michael Brower
5424 SE Gladstone Street
Portland, OR 97206
503.753.8325

Dear Mr. Brown!

I know you see 'the worst in people' like, every day. Can I convince you (even for a little while) that I'm trying to show 'the good in people' with Brian Miller and www.stardragons.org? I hope I can. With that woman in Florida, (a very nice woman) calling me, I think she said that you can 'save me' some money–but this is my state at present (attached). I need this site, need it desperately.

I'm struggling to pay for the $144 per month that my website is charging us. It is very hard. I'm trying to put a PayPal account up on the site right now. It would be so, so good if you could forbear that (devastating) $144 per month–at least until I've got some money built up in that account. I'm trying to do the same thing with www.jmbrower. com with that PayPal account. I'm long since retired, suffering a major, debilitating stroke.

I've got this book I'm working (feverishly) on, The Saurian Theory of Anarchy. It will be ready in five months. Can you not take out $144 a month? That would really help me! I hope it works! Thank you!

Warmly,
J. Michael Brower

I looked at J. Michael Brower like he was a loon, but he was very serious looking. He was in command of the classics, but I could see some awesome holes in his fragile knowledge. I did read another email, just laughing quietly:

Sharon Rowlands   April 8, 2020
CEO, The Web Company
13861 Sunrise Valley Drive, #300
Herndon, Virginia 20171

Dear Ms. Rowlands!

"The War came close today. I would like to end it. For a little while, if I can. You want to end it, don't you? For a little while? For a night?" This is from Burt Lancaster, in Castle Keep. This is a book by William Eastlake, and it touched me so much, I ordered it off of ebay.com. The book was as witty as the movie—now, I'm dealing with COVID-19 (SARS-2, for the technical-minded). So far, no infection (although, I think I've already had it!).

So I needed, and definitely wanted, to thank you for supporting www.stardragons.org and I couldn't find the 'time,' to be appreciative. I'm not ignorant—I listened to the writing career of D.C. Fontana and I can't 'write' like Dorothy, and that, never (see https://www.youtube.com/watch?v=qjGYRTQma60). I think I will disappoint you, but here are my chapters (attached). Dorothy Catherine Fontana died last December, but maybe she can sorta continue in my reedition of 'these several' dragon-stars. I'm going to try it. Thank you for your ideas!

Yours,
J. Michael Brower
503.753.8325

I was nearly rolling on the ground with merriment at this "blanket email":

January 2019

Quite obviously, you like dragons—me, too! The 'dragons' in my seven books, This is my third or fourth letter to you concerning my Brian Miller series. Now, I have to announced Brian Miller: Joan of Arc and the Dragon-Stars—published, as I told you, this year, you can get it by typing in the same, on Google, id est, your search engine. It's okay that you don't really respond to my 'scribbling pieces', my fountain-pen correspondence any-old-way. I think most people are in shock about my 'bad writing' (or worse). My wife says my writing is wrong, lousy, shitty, evil, a total annoyance, noxious, foul, rotten, shockingly boring, burdensome, and, in one word, just bad! It's very nice to have such loving support, but that's not my point. The thing is, *I'm possessed*! I had to write about Joan of Arc because Mark Twain and Bernard Shaw and a host of others wrote about her. Not that I'm in that "class" for writers—and that's the whole problem! I'm an anarchist in so far as I detest 'class' in all its colors. I'm a socialist, though, because people have to stick together—and I'm a Champaign socialist/communist because I embrace and celebrate President Roosevelt's Social Security system. This book, given its notes (all important), is really what I think (or there-abouts, soon to be confronted with <u>its own</u> antithesis, anon!). And, (at once) this is my <u>weakest</u> book to date. I know that. It took about a year to write, and I know the real weaknesses, hell, I wrote it! But, like one of my kids says, if "they" really like it, 'they' will just <u>steal it</u> from me. So, I'm planning to do a Youtube. com series soon: I have to figure out how to edit stuff...of course, I feel estranged, abstracted, and really alienated from my work...but...here it is, here I am! (...won't you send me an angel?)—that's from the Scorpions (ahem, giving credit where it's due, which might not be <u>my</u> due!):

It was just *visions*, that's the answer to the question ??why?? creating my series of Brian Miller books. I've been a freelance writer and got paid to write. This is what Dan Cragg said, and that's how you can tell a writer—if he gets paid for what he's doing, that is, writing. He taught me that, but Dan always wrote <u>with</u> someone else (and, as you know, 'Brian Miller' and 'Harry Potter' have the same number of letters in their names, speaking of 'true things.' And I get 'Post-Truth' <u>good</u> in a note in <u>Joan of Arc and the Dragon-Stars</u>, too). Thing is, I met Brian Miller when I was a teenager, long before J. K. Rowling wrote about Harry Potter in her famous 'unemployment.' Because that's what happened, Joanne couldn't get a publisher in England, and everyone was very dismissive of her. Now, we know different. For me, I've gone <u>through</u> five publishers. That might be my epitaph. What I really need is a reply, and please, please buy some of my books! Thank you for your ideas.

Warmly Yours,
J. Michael Brower. 503.753.8325 www.stardragons.org

And this one, just as a little bitter-biter, pathetic that J. Michael Brower thinks that such an exalted human 'personage' would ever read one of his begging letters:

Jamie Dimon   June 26, 2020
CEO and Chairman
270 Park Avenue
New York, NY. 10005

J. Michael Brower
5424 SE Gladstone Street
Portland, OR 97206
503.753.8325

Dear Mr. Dimon!

My circumstances have not changed since I last wrote you. I've been charged at least $1755.48 just THIS YEAR from Web.com, and I'm just OUT that, right now! This Web.com company is ripped me off big time. I hope you can do something about this, I really, really need you help as a starving artist! I have documents for your records. Thank you for your ideas.

Sincerely,
J. Michael Brower

What a moron, what a supreme sucker, what a naïve simpleton! I couldn't believe that Brian Miller was wasting his time with this simpering, apologetic belletrist. Michael believed in anything provided it was dumb, and I'm quoting the late Gore Vidal saying that there was "no lie so great that you can't get an American to believe it, particularly if it's bitchy and mean." In short, he was a fool with money (which is a sin, anyway). I just had to cry out, in my dragon voice so I could be heard, the other two humans were laughing like lunatics together (they'd raided Katrina's 'kitty' so there was wine, vodka, and screwballs, and they were legion, with booze-jiggers for the miscellaneous challenges these humans set up for themselves, simply unbelievable!):

Dumb, obese, mentally demolished and utterly smashed is no way to go through life, J. Michael Brower!

—I think, in reading these shittily-designed emails, that you wrote "you" when you meant "your," right? All kinds of mistakes and middle and mis-sentences, anywhere and everywhere. Never mind that, hey, what's this little phrase, "Thank you for your ideas" mean, Mr. Laughable Scribbler?

Both humans stopped talking, turning like drunken schoolboys, both had a half a bag on right then. Michael looked around at his emails scattered about, with some chagrin, mimicking a sense of comportment addressing a dragon, I guess, sobering up quickly.

—Ah, well, uh, Terminus, my liege-n-lord, it's kind of a loose quote from Joseph Stalin when he was making the case for collectivization to party officials, and he wasn't interested in 'the facts' he was interested in 'what is to be done?' and no one had any meaningful suggestions, they just had complaints. So "Thank you for your ideas" is just saying if you have any ideas, thank you; criticism I'll just address preconsciously or maybe subconsciously, with human backs to the wall, my lord. You can't really become a party liner, because, then, your back would be against the wall. And, well, you'd get shot. I mean, if you're a human, that's a big (and final) deal, my noble dragon-star king.

—Ah-ha. You made a lot of other mistakes in these books, too!

—True, my lord. However, I'm still walking out of here with $600,000, jes' sayin'.

—Another question human: You place an exclamation point at the end of the person you address, so, _explanation_?

—My lord, that's the Russian way to address folks in letters, I guess.

—Yeah, lot of good that did you, Master Belletrist?

Stupid, fat, drunk, and editor-less is no way to go through life, J. Michael Brower! What a waste of a person-opolis.

—Did anything come of all these letters, Michael?

—My lord: That has yet to be seen.

At that, I left them, as they childishly chatted away. I can see why J. Michael Brower is just looking for an honorable way out. He's like Leon Trotsky, Christopher Hitchens, Chris Hedges and Gore Vidal all rolled up into a pudgy, fetid sausage, and, looking at his erstwhile 'thinkers,' it can't end well. Not my affair, really, consider me for flushing the "human condition" down any local toilet, throwing in drugs and booze, there's a Trinity for you.

My affair: I'm off to get my companion into the mini-castle that Sheeta Miyazaki deserves somewhere on Crocodilia!

APPENDIX ONE
LARRY KING VS. THE DRAGON-STARS

TOTALLY IRONICALLY (AT LEAST, TO ME) AND TO OTHER SAURIANS everywhere and everywhen, Larry King did an interview with Littorian, Lord of the Lizardanians, and his 'heir apparent' Soreidian a couple of days after the epic football game. The Black World weapons set this up and King was very game. Soreidian was exhausted, even though he had Lizardanian help with his injuries. This was after the saurian football game, which kept them fighting for three and a half hours. In all sparring matches in saurian history, none had lasted so long. Both reptilians, exhausted beyond words, featured Littorian a little brighter, a little stronger, than Soreidian.

TABLE LENGTH IN LARRY'S OFFICE WAS A BIG DEAL, AT LEAST TO THE Black World swords. First, the saurians could sit like Sphinxes, as they were used to. King didn't want to sit at any table other than his mahogany arrangement and with his favorite chair. The leaves were Australian Buloke wood, and still the reptilians were advised to take it gingerly, on the table itself. They had to put four leaves in the table to expand it out. So, the table was increased fourfold, just to accommodate their massive forms.

—On Larry King Now, a special, our soon-to-be-gone to-the-stars dragons take a break with us here to talk about their football game and answer a few of your questions. Littorian, the Lord of the Lizardanians, and his second, Soreidian, have joined me tonight. Good evening to you, my illustrious dragon-stars!

Soreidian was relaxed, sitting on a great Iranian rug which crisscrossed the carpet Littorian was seated on. Both Lizardanians were so tall, King had to look up to make eye contact, even with them sitting like a Sphinx.

—I'm glad to be here and what relaxing carpets you have. I'm just too exhausted to notice anything else, hit me with an asteroid just to wake me up, please. You've heard of foreshadowing; well, this is back-shadowing, that's something dragon-esque for you.

Littorian followed up, also at his ease.

—I like my carpet, too, Larry. Very good, you must have coordinated with Brian to provide such accommodations. Maybe I'll go to Iran, just before we leave, I'll put my companion on it. It's society that brings you these kinds of thoughts. Maybe that society will have Iranian rugs that I can bring home? This rug is so cool!

—Speaking of these Iranian rugs, which are predominately red, we are speaking together tonight just after the football game, and I've never seen more of a bloody fight in my life!

Soreidian just laughed.

—Yes, I guess the blood and gore was fun, and I understand the Black World weapons have cleaned it all up, and that's good. They paid out a lot of money for the 'inconvenience' of the game, too. I guess looking for sunken ships has some benefits. Tiperia won the day, I should have known that I was outmatched mentally.

—Don't beat yourself up over that (just leave that to me), you just try to be Tiperia's lover, then you'll see.

Larry King had to provide some background.

—Now Tiperia is—

—My lover. She's been that way for eons. I can't get enough of her, and she is the only one for me. For instance, we had a session on Lizardania, recently, and there was an Olympic size swimming pool that we filled up with our—

—Uh, so, Soreidian, do you think—

—Tiperia outmatched me, during the football game. Let's not hear the details of this epic deleteriousness, this is a family affair on social media, let's have a little deference. And that's enough said on this love affair, lest I snatch your head off, behave yourself, didn't the companions brief you?

—Oh, yes, that's okay, because—

—I really don't have the energy to break-up Tiperia and Littorian. That would get the Universe out of order, and for this anarchist, that's all the order I want. Too, I'm not for including a circle around anarchy. The circle means order, and I'm not taking any orders from any source. Still, right now, I'm feeling very weak and if your military wants a re-re-do, I'd be challenged. We aren't God Almighty, we're just 'gods' with a very, very small 'g'. And I'm not too dumb to know that humans can defeat the dragon-stars too. I think going up against Littorian over that football game, humbled me. I can't believe I'm saying this but sparring matches don't have the level of appeal in my mind, that they once did. I'm for leaving Earth, and will, but for now, well, I've worked it all out of my system, sparring with Littorian. I really respect him, not his decisions, but the physical Littorian, as Tiperia says, 'You can't go no better.' Wish I'd known that before the football game. I'll have to tell you, Larry, I was feeling so tired, I was thinking about asking for a respite. I didn't. You see, I knew my challenger asked for no quarter and definitely gave none. I am so hopelessly ready to leave! I'm glad Littorian will be with me, I respect his prodigious strength.

—In the interests of time let's turn to questions from our audience. From Johnson City, Tennessee!

—I appreciate your saving the world, but didn't you endanger it all in the first place?

Littorian handled the question draconically.

—Yeah, in a word: You can't win them all. Best learn that. Humans were a factor; you'll be the judge whether it was for good or ill.

Larry responded.

—You mean human teenagers were a factor, that should give the adults some comfort. This next one is from Chicago, Illinois, yes, ma'am?

—I know that there are only 30 companions, but didn't Brian Miller make it so there are more? I understand there is a new ninth planet, replacing Pluto, with all kinds of dragons on it? Like 5,000 dragons? So, if you're thinking there is some kind of black hole at the edge of the solar system, the dragon-stars will take care of it?

—May I, Larry?

—Oh, please, Soreidian, you're play (so to post-football speak).

—Like Littorian said, you can't win them all. That's my humble-time, Larry.

—Ah-huh. What wisdom! Next call, from Biloxi, Mississippi, sir?

—Yeah, these Lizzies are as strong as Superman and, like, everyone that doesn't exist today! We are done for, aren't we, like they will attack us? I'm just trying to reach out.

—Either of you dragon-stars want to take on that insightful comment?

Soreidian just giggled.

—That would be true, if it wasn't completely false. My whole thing was to leave, with Littorian, with our companions. I value my safety more than I value your time, Larry. Thing is, about Superman, you could separate him from his noggin, then you'd have a superhero without a head. That'd be boring, something that deters dragons.

—This one is from Lakeville, Minnesota, no less. Ma'am?

—Hello? Gosh, it's an honor to be talking to dragons, wow. Can they come to some of our colleges up here and give a talk?

Both saurians responded instantly.

—Really not!

—Why not?

The saurians were dumbfounded. Littorian drummed out.

—Ma'am, maybe you should read <u>Brian Miller & the Twins of Triton</u>, I think then you'd understand. In a word, dragon's shouldn't be here.

—Then why is Brian Miller making sure that dragons will be here.

Littorian grumbled.

—Brian Miller is going with me, off this planet, out of this solar system, and…uh, a long way away!

Larry intervened.

—I think that getting into a debate with Littorian will be like debating Donald Trump. It couldn't end well.

—Well, thanks a lot, Larry, and total yuck, and I mean bigly! Brian Miller is his own person, and I'd interview him, Larry, if you want to.

—I'd rather interview you two saurians. From Cleveland, Ohio, we have another question, please!

—Thanks, Larry, and good evening. I only heard the football game on the radio. I'm sure everyone wants to know why Littorian didn't just finish off Soreidian with a sparring match, either in the game or just after?

At that, Soreidian perked up.

—Could I answer that question, Larry?

—Sure thing.

—Thank you and just so. Mercy is all. If a saurian sees the soft white underbelly of a fellow reptilian, that is, when he is totally finished off, I think it's the higher sophistication of mercy that stays the hand of the victor. I think that mercy was shown to me by Littorian, and I'm not sure why. Really, I was defeated, and this is a remark that a dragon would roast a human-whole for saying, but it was true. At the end of the game I was a mess to saurian society. Littorian took everything and anything I had and still stood above me. It takes a lot of humility (but no humanity, yuck) to admit it, but Littorian does deserve the so-called throne of Lord of the Lizardanians, whatever that consists of.

—And me now?

—Please, Lord of the Lizardanians?

—It wasn't me. I would have finished him. It was Brian Miller.

—Your notable (and notorious) companion?

—The same all around.

Soreidian sighed.

—Great. Now I owe Brian again! This never ends.

—It will now. Thank you both for visiting, and not breaking anything and you can keep the Iranian rugs, I know that you are dragons and would take them anyway!

APPENDIX TWO

STAR DRAGON IN FLIGHT AND OUR MARVELOUS SPECTACULAR

MY ANGELIC, SO TOTALLY RIPPED, MEGA-SERPENT CLAREINA GAZED over the vast amount of grass in the Everglades. Asking Larascena if she'd 'loan' me to Clareina for an evening and it was agree to. Lara reminded me that she'd ask for <u>twice</u> an evening liaison on my return. I smiled at her, while Clare winked, and we flew off.

The dragoness turned East, rather quickly, and then gestured to a field, her wings folded in the twilight. The ocean, just over the tall grass a subdued blue. Clare considered thoughtfully.

—See those? Those fireflies? I've seen sights on other worlds, of course, but I haven't seen what this planet is capable of producing, so my jury is out. Clouds, I'd like to see them on display, alright? I'd like a companions' thought on all of this, not just my husband's feelings?

—Sure, Clare and stated quickly, your pleasure and my satisfaction are running neck and neck; and your neck looks vitally and majestically suck-ability!

—That's suck-able, hold your swift, horney horses until we leave, let's run with the tension. Remember, curiosity killed the cat, but satisfaction brought him back with a raging third leg.

—Sorry, Clare, that was my angry, votive Clydesdale, down boy, nay, nay. I've got that particular beast under (some) control.

—I think now we're talking turkey, maybe you can get your massive bowling ball rocks off riding me, sounds like fun, I think my green back will be proteined up, right?

I prepared to ride the dragoness. Her muscled wings emerged from her back, immense sinews and her sleek scales moving slightly, giving me a cushioned seat. Being so close to her, I tried to see her as just giving me a ride; oh such, such impossibilities, as my hands manipulated here, there and everywhere.

—My lady, I'll keep my loins in check. If you are hungry, with the sea right there, we can go after a great white shark with fancy tartar sauce?

I liked to be funny around Clare, a failing I have (you probably don't think it's funny, you had to be there).

—I could break a great white shark's backbone like you squishing a grape, and do you have some tartar sauce?

I played around at the beach, looking for shells. Clare was ready to get down to business, but she delayed a second.

—I've a question for you, Brian Miller Human, just before we get started today?

—Go ahead, my lady.

—What are the ten books that have most influenced your thinking, my Brian?

—Oh, I couldn't 'take' just ten books, my lady; there are books by Richard Bach, like <u>Jonathan Livingston Seagull</u>, things by Jack London, Bernard Shaw, the Joan of Arc series (at least 50 books there), so many pamphlets, things on Oliver Cromwell, I've had a correspondence with Noam Chomsky, and that Leftist literature, my anti-capitalism volumes, many hundreds of them and—

—Let me re-state my question. If I draconically took you away from the little Earth, and you could only bring ten books with you, what are they?

—Ten, well, I, I've just got to give you just ten names? I mean, there are so many books, by John Spargo, John Work, Olive Schreiner and—

—That's it my child! Oh, come now, I understand that your female Black Sword, who will be heartily employed, anon, is bringing all the work with you, tens of thousands of volumes, no, just your top ten, come on and give it to me now!

—But there are books by Trotsky, like <u>My Life</u>, and Maurice Cornforth has a set of three books, and then <u>War Is A Racket</u>, by Major General Smedley Butler, and those three volumes that are under—

—Nah, come, ten, now!

The Lizardanian was so Velociraptor-y right then, I just had to say whatever came to my mind. If there are books, like the classics: Dostoyevsky, Aristotle, Homer, Hugo, Orwell, Conrad, Poe, Lovecraft, Milton, well, they do have a place for me, to be sure. Then, I was thinking of 'things-dramatic.'

—Okay, my lady, not in any order of what's important, and we are just walking on the beach, and that reminds me of Poe's great novel, <u>The Narrative of Arthur Gordon Pym of Nantucket</u>, it was published in the summer of 1838, and this was Poe's only novel so—

—I'm waiting!

—Alright, my esteemed lady. I was just going to say that Jack London, Edgar Allan Poe and Robert E. Howard didn't make it past 40 years old but set that aside. I believe these books are: <u>War-What For?</u> by George R. Kirkpatrick; <u>Woman and Labor</u> by Olive Schreiner; <u>Bolshevism: The Enemy of Political and Industrial Democracy</u>, John Spargo; <u>Flying Serpents and Dragons: The Story of Mankind's Reptilian Past</u>, R.A. Boulay; <u>Notes for a Journal</u>, Maxim Litvinov; <u>The ABC of Anarchism</u>, Alexander Berkman; <u>The ABC of Communism</u>, by Nikolai Bukharin; <u>What's So and What</u>

<u>Isn't</u>, by John M. Work; <u>Rule by Secrecy</u>, Jim Marrs; <u>The Intelligent Woman's Guide To Socialism and Capitalism</u> by Bernard Shaw; <u>Merchants of Death,</u> by H.C. Engelbrecht and F.C. Hanighen and—

—Huh-huh, that's enough. Wow, such odd titles.

—I was going to mention <u>The Washing of the Spears</u>, by Donald R. Morris and <u>The Rebel</u> by Albert Camus, but I wanted to be in keeping with your top ten, and there is <u>Woman and Socialism</u> by August Bebel, but in keeping with—

—Tut, tut, I think I've heard enough titles. Your first one is most particular and peculiar. <u>War: What For?</u> What's that about?

—My lady, it's written in 1909 or 1910, four or five years before World War One, and it talks about the 99% having issues with the 1%, and socialism, and it's always been that way, I mean, the poor against the rich, a few humans always dominate the many. Thing is, when the 99% gets to govern then you get, well, I guess that never happens, but like that guy that wrote that thing on Rome, Edward Gibbon, said, "History is indeed little more than the register of the crimes, follies, and misfortunes of mankind."

—Doesn't that make you kinda cynical?

—What doesn't, my lady, if you are dealing with history? Unless you are 'outside of your mind' like the Nazis or the drunk Russians. Only then, at first, just at the first part of a revolution, you have a hopeful chance: The Germans made the Volkswagen and the autobahn, and the Russians equalized things, at the beginning between men and women, and there was, very briefly, 'all power to the soviets, or 'counsels,' but then Stalin came in. The anarchists tried to assassinate Lenin, and then, things started to go south. Those people couldn't handle power (well, they did, and the Holocaust and World War Two were just part of their answers) everything breaks down over time, you have Mussolini and Hitler and they all eventuate into dictatorship just to 'get things done.' If dragons were there, it could have been different.

—Gods with a small 'g,' hear that? I've got some books for you to read on Lizardania, and they aren't so 'cynical' believe me; they have the joy of dragon-star life inside them.

—Bring it on, my queen.

—First, this. My weapons, come and listen.

Clare whisked over my weapons, one sword, two knives and two hatchets and her own. Clare had one knife loaned out, so nine weapons pensively awaited their "order suggestions."

—I've a little game we can—

—Are we going to look the world-over for trolls, gnomes, spinners, maybe some meteors, transient luminous events, Clare, are we, are we?

—…play. Stand by, my excitable, garish knife. You'll have access to my incredible mind (and yes, I say so!) and via my telepathy, the things I need to see will be communicated to all, right? Pixies, halos, blue jets, right, and so much more. Good, and at this time, your fully briefed. This time of the year is perfect for warping through clouds, anywhere around the world. And warp I will! Our weapons have their assignments. And we will see everything. Okay, be off, go, shoo, shooed, and shooing!

The huge beast turned to me, smiling (I mean, really smiling).

—This will be fantastic for all the weapons, Brian Miller Human. All of them have the constant craving to be the first one back to report on my Bucket List. I wonder if my weapons will return first?

A knife reported earliest, one of mine.

—Oh, oh, Clareina, my Lizardanian, oh! I have an aurora in Antarctica, you'll be pleased.

The massive serpent warped over to the South Pole in about three seconds, arriving like any Dragon-Whirling Dervish.

—You alright, my inattentive husband, didn't leave something behind in the sand, somewhere?

—Oh, sure, I didn't need my innards anyway, they are on a beach in Florida, I'm okay!

In shock, I observed the greens and blues, starlight all around, the sun almost set.

—Now, I'll show you something. Immediately, she flashed her muscled wings.

—What do you see?

—Well, nothing, Clare. I do see the aurora down below, and to the left, it's so beautiful and majestic. As you know, natural bullshit just comes with being a person, Clare.

—We are right in the greens you just saw, it's not green now, is it?

—No, my empress, it isn't.

—That's the thing: If you get too close to something, its value is suspended to you, things lose the luster, right? The birds 'singing' in the park; but what are they saying, really? Stay out of my territory, other birds! You'll see at the rainbow.

—The rainbow, my lady?

—Oh, sure, you'll see then!

They watched the aurora, a very great one, for a few minutes, greens, and reds, purples, light blues.

—Charged particles from the sun, you see, strike atoms in the Earth's little canopy. That causes electrons in the atoms to move to a higher-energy level. When the electrons drop back into a lower energy state, they release photons of light. Now you know why you can't physically touch it.

Then she made a comment that shuttered me.

—Hey, pretty good plan on getting with Katrina and Teresian for going back in time and establishing Wysteria as your new ninth planet, just as 'the saurians won the day,' in motivating you to leave Earth, right? I mean your tinkering around with our dragon-esque plans; you made a 'side arrangement' on the vulnerable Wysterian to use her vast amount of dragon-star-energy to return to the past and get her planet back. And that despite the zombie-affair that she screwed up with Kat? So, this new Wysterian planet couldn't permit a black hole or a comet, or whatever else from beating the shit out of your Earth, but for their own saurian welfare? Well and most cynically done. An accursed human genius must be responsible for this elaborate plan. I bet that wily Russian Katrina helped you there, say that isn't true and I'll eat your mouth (and I might do that anyway)? And then, for insurance, you arranged with Turinian, the new Lord of the Crocodilians, to get into some kind of peace-deal here on Earth, too? You were enemies with him once? Even gooder, and that with almost 14,000 nuclear warheads in the world? You cut-short World War Three, right, with dragon-might? You couldn't blow yourselves up with dragons right 'next door' on their new world of Wysteria? You humans can take on gods, and deviousness alone will do, right Brian? And then, I bet, you planned to get more and more dragon-stars companioned off, a double insurance for you there, the dragons would prevent war because they'd 'feel' for their teenage humans. And you'd team up the entire Wysterian planet with them, 5,000 dragons, isn't that their population? War can't be the same: If everyone has a nuke, the rich and the poor will be blown to bits. And you'll do something about that, and you can't care what that is, even using your position and reptilian friends, right? Uh-huh and we are the monsters on Earth? Saurian's aren't the monsters, really. You know, you're the monster here!

—That's a lot to unpack, but let's just leave that suitcase packed to the full. This monster is married to you, my dear Clare. There is a black-washing cruel terrorism lurking within the human soul, my Clare, can a dragon handle it or reject it?

—I'll do neither. Ah, Brian, again, we are not God Almighty, just your neighborhood gods, and that, with reason and you know how to defeat any dragon: With love in your heart. You see? I've got a good feeling about this!

Another weapon arrived, a knife from Clare's arsenal.

—Elves! I've got Elves over here, order number three, gang way, gang way, letta well-meaning knife through! And when you have an Elf, you have Sprites, too, so this is a double count for me. The location is Tornado Alley, I'll give you the GPS right now, the coordinates and then we can—

Clare was immediately gone to the exact site, in Oklahoma. A powerful Triple Sprite sequence was commencing, and even Clare was fascinated. The Sprite illuminated, just then, like a mangrove tree. She appeared way over the lighting just at the right time.

Over the Sprites arena, Clare bellowed out, very dragonesquely: *!!!All Times Standing Still!!!*

And just like, time and every-single-thing did stand still.

Clare was instructive, gazing at the furtive clouds, and secretly excited that her magic had worked the first time, though she tried to be matter-of-course, in her speaking. It was so, just as I've said, so quiet just then, it was like a dream (only, it wasn't a dream when you were living it, really living it, only after, did you realize it was a dream, only then!)

—Look at that huge jellyfish-cloud, three of them, discharging, you see? These are crawlers, trolls and tendrils climbing up the sprites? And look at that, a Green Ghost appears, just after that far left-hand sprite disappeared. I caught it in the middle of my Time Stand Still spell. That is 'Green emissions from excited Oxygen in Sprite Tops', so ghosts, right? It's all in keeping with the fantasy-nature of the whole thing. And of that, almost everything is here, the pixies, gnomes, hisses, whistlers, chorus, ball lighting, St. Elmo's fire, oh, we will see it all, my human. Look, there is a blue jet or a starter blue jet rising up? We are now looking, from this vantage, into the Mesosphere and Stratosphere. Very awesome, and I wonder how many people know about these events? You should see them on some other planets. I'll just let you soak it all in, enjoy!

I was in awe and so-many-shucks at the incredible event. I wished I could exchange a few words with this mini-god beneath me, and I just couldn't find the words. The tendrils went down to the lower atmosphere, and my camera and video recorder taped it all. I wondered if this wasn't "Stairway to Heaven," right in front of me. Clare pointed out with her huge, eagle eyes the intricate patterns of the event.

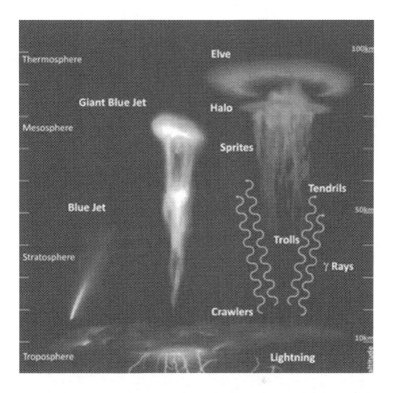

—It's all charged particles, negative and positive, nitrogen molecules in the atmosphere. A sprite is Stratospheric Perturbations mesospheric Resulting from Intense Thunderstorm Electrification. It gives off blue, red and all kinds of colors when you're away from it, just like a rainbow does, when the light hits it right, and there is the halo overhead, see? It's all oh-hum for yours truly, for sure, there was some power I was up against, and I didn't expect it's strength, but that's just because I'm young, and sorta inexperienced. That's just between me and you, my human husband, a dragon thinks they are the world (or more) in terms of power, sad, as this football game proved, that they are not. All the same, I sorted it, and then some. You weren't shocked, like physically, were you? Sometimes seeing things at a distance is better, and more loveable, that seeing them up close with all their flaws and imperfections. It's only with the heart that one can see clearly; what's essential is invisible to the eye. That's from <u>The Little Prince</u>, and I have respect for Antoine de Saint-Exupery. For the coup-de-scissors, let's go and find me a double or a triple rainbow, come on weapons, I'm telepathing to you and I'm waiting, let's go, let's go!

All the weapons chimed in at once, seeking to outdo their comrade rivals, thinking up all kinds of crazy stuff to say (or think!).

I have a huge rope of a rainbow, in Australia!

I have a double rain-bow-shot in Papua New Guinea!

I have a real nice double rain-Pterosaurs in Mozambique!

I have a triple-rain-facial-bow in Angola, Africa, off the coast, Atlantic ocean, here's the GPS and coordinates, it won't last long, it's peaking, peaking! And I have a Gustnado too, you know, a little mini-tornado, as an added bonus!

—Angola, here I come, watch out world!

A huge, anti-wave washed up on the Benguela Beach, Angola, crashing out to sea, of course, created by Clare. It was a stormy day, that's for sure.

—Yup, there it is! There's the termination point. You know what's at the end of that rainbow out there in Western Angola?

—Just let me guess, like, a treasure chest?

—You got it. Oh, you spoiled it for me, for shame! Hey, look at that, Brian, there may *be* someplace over the rainbow, see?

—Where, my—?

Something happened, and I felt that there wasn't a dragon underneath me at all, then Clare returned. It only happened for a second.

The knife making the discovery showed up, one of Clare's. In fact, he was the only knife she had, loaning the other to Daenerys Targaryen.[2]

—Oh, oh, I have the coordinates, all is prepared, right Clare?

—Yeah, yeah, don't give anything away, troublesome little knife, you're lucky I didn't lend you out, where is it?

---

[2] See _A Dragon-Star Lives Forever (More)_, pg. 59

Coordinates given in flashing telepathy, and then, in an equal-flash, Clare was only 50 feet off the ground, looking down.

—Ta-dah!

There, next to some Adansonia and baobab trees, was a massive chest right out of <u>Treasure Island</u>. Something occurred to me then.

—Oh, I get it. You located a sunken ship in the Atlantic Ocean, disappeared to go get that treasure chest and then reappeared under me, correct, my lady?

—An got a miscellaneous skeleton or two in the process, along with a case of flintlocks! That was a rare find, because the wood would have been washed away. It was preserved in a kinda vacuum. You should see them, against than Adansonia tree, that giant case of firearms? They're almost new. That was the real *ta-dah*, there! I haven't looked inside that chest, should be fun, yes? No?

—I think they should say at the end of the rainbow is a chest, if you are riding a dragon. Can we see it all, Clare?

Instantly, we hovered over the sight, and we dropped down. I went after the chest immediately, and I was fired on by a machine gun! At least ten outlaws surrounded the place, after seeing the dragon "make a deposit."

—Oh, my gosh, human pirates! Quick, the flintlocks, Brian, hurry, you're our only defense, help, I'm just a helpless lady, help, help! A staccato of flintlock-fire should be your answer, go get 'em, Brian Miller Human!

Clare was feeling beyond-Superwoman right then, the bullets bouncing and ricocheting off her heavily muscled frame, disregarding the eldritch portent of the moment. The weapons thought this was a laughable situation, too.

The Black World weapons, humorously, took the time to ping and glance slugs that would have ended me, too, so many where aimed for me. A few impacts I could survive, but I don't know about a whole slew of them. The guerrillas or pirates—or whoever they were—didn't approach the saurian but felt good about taking pot-shots at the both of us, aiming for my head, mostly. My good-natured hatchet (and one with the restored soul) helped me with the wardrobe-of-flintlocks, opening them lickety-split for ready use, in our Clare-designed Laurel and Hardy comedy routine.

The hatchet then thought to me, just like Flounder in Animal House:

Oh, boy, is this great!

Inside where 12 Scottish Murdoch pistols and 12 muskets, all from around the 1770s. They'd been in the ocean for over 200 years, so I wasn't sure they'd even discharge. They must have invented some kind of vacuum-circumstance for them, because they were in great shape. What use flintlocks would be against today's rifle bullets tinkering around, was a mystery to me. I thought desperately.

Okay, pan, hammer, frizzen, frizzen spring, jaws from the flint (is the flint wet, or will it break off?), then cock the hammer back, ball, powder, rammer, full cock, aim, fire, I got this, but how do I, you know, load this son of a bitch anyway?

Then something occurred to me.

Yeah, the dragon is in control of this situation, she's cheapening me here, she can control any of these guys, why is she being so helpless right now? Well, never mind, I've got three or four of these tinker toys ready, come on, and aim low!

I started with a musket. A villain was firing at me about 30 yards away.

—Halt and put that rifle down, and it's my life, it never ends!

A hail of .30 caliber bullets was my answer.

I fired and there was a hell of a boom. I hit the dude square in the chest. "I hated to have to kill them all, but they had to be taught a lesson," ode to that old cartoon, Ralph Phillips. Ah, those were the days. Why did they make only two Ralph Phillips' thingy-things?

The ball I fired was a .40 caliber and could put anyone down. I was proud of my accuracy. Then the pirate got up again. Not disabled, he picked up his AK-47 and fired again. My Black World swords blocked every incoming bullet. Clare shooed them away, wanting, wishing to be hit! My other weapons were feeling bored.

I grabbed both Murdock pistols and fired. Two chests, two pirates, perfect hits. And up they both rose, after a second or two.

—Clare, I could use a little help!

—They have bullet-proof vests on you silly simian simpleton. I'm thinkin' for ideas, my human. I guess I have to do all the work myself, ho-hum. Just check this physicality-action-out and compare it to all the fights in The Raid, okay? Wow, I loved that series, good that you introduced me to that, watch this!

Then Clare went to work, waiving back all the weapons. She went to town on the ten pirates and what an extreme, violent, and, in parts, sexual site to see! Clare towered above them, goading them to take down a Lizardanian. The rifles were thrown down; the whole group approached the reptilian with knives-akimbo. I thought if guns don't work, what are knives going to do?

All the action took less than two minutes. Clare's massively cobblestoned abdominals actually pushed people aside, mushing them into trees, and this happened to a bunch of ruffians. The reptilian destroyed men's bodies like they were paper mâché, lifting them up, breaking their spines like the Predator, only worse, devouring men like ice cream on a very sunny day.

—I'm going to crack your femur bones into painful quarters, and then we will get started, right?

She broke the scofflaws backs, arms, legs, until all were moaning on the ground. A pirate ended up backwards, as she lifted him up with ease, then made the back of his head come together with his Achilles heel, enough said there, and it was a terrible sight to see, as his chest and stomach literally blew up in a huge field of guts, the saurian force was so great. She bulged out all her massive strength, flexing incredibly, just for me, her arms looked like Mount Olympus. One guy she just lightly picked up like an unrulily baby with a doll, and then shook him with ultra-extreme vigor until all his bones were literally broken. He was reduced to pinata-status, wrecked candy inside. When the suspended pirate hit "tube man" status, Clare, a mammoth, spouting Chernobyl of estrogen, the pirate all wobbly inside, she dismissively flicked him into an Adansonia tree, literally breaking him in half, scattering his fragmented bones. Another erstwhile fellow, witnessing, was just about to scream, and she taloned and clawed him to way-over-death, like a great, practically invisible, slicer out of the movie Cube. He didn't even know it was happening until way too late. That forlorn pirate just fell to the ground in bloody chunks. Another scofflaw, about to scream at the macabre scene, had his mouth open all the way. Clare maneuvered a left hand, right down his throat, emerging at the man's kippering, jiggling junk. Clare speared her fingers around this organ, and ripped a hole at the man's loins, then completely reversed his body, inside-outside! I've never seen a human being abused so, and I thought magic, maybe Black Magic, was involved. The others I won't say what happened to them, but one guy ended up a bloody tennis ball, crushed down with her iron hands, blood, viscera, organs, everything, matted together in her talented, but vicious claws. Then she literally swept her hands and claws clean of all the blood, in a frightening, and liberal, sheen. All the Black World weapons were stunned looking on, totally frightened. They'd cleaned up such reptilian violence before, but never had they actually seen the sausage being freshly made in a powerful saurian grip.

Then she leapt over to me then, yanking up, her 50 plus inch biceps around my neck, squeezing politely and subtly insistently, she was really wrapped around me, so-entirely. I was conflicted in my feelings, I didn't know whether to resist or gratefully concede to Clare's awesome, Lizardanian-consuming, crushing power. I saw right in her golden, silver and green eyes, mesmerized. I was so totally hers and she knew it, entirely. I was mastered, just like a Queen's victim on any chessboard (anywhere) or anyone married for 30 years or more.

—And that's the reason why we can't have dragons running around on Earth, right, my dear? Otherwise, you humans would just go all to molecular-pieces, see?

She really laughed and released me.

—We crave mystery because there is none really left, at least not physically speaking. But I'm not a mere Crocodilian, remember that, my kindness abounds.

Clare let the pirates suffer, but just a little while, and then cured them all with her astounding magic. Knowing they were profoundly defeated the simpering pirates left the treasure chest, scampering off, lowered heads like any just-fired butlers. Clare stretched, did an iron, pulsing muscle check all-around (which, despite her violence, I really liked). As the Lizardanian meticulously checked the mountainous layers of her left, cascading bicep, she looked at me warmly.

—At least I got a little bit of a work-out? See, I let them all live, aren't I great? Feel so totally free to be overly obsequious, prepare to worship me, right about now. Waiting. Now?

I was otherwise distracted by her muscle check, as she casually snapped the lock off the chest.

—Oh my God, look at the gold and silver!

—I guess it means something to you, doesn't it?

—Can I replace my kitty with it, my lady?

—You're low on whatever it is, what's it called, huh, money?

—J. Michael Brower came out with $100,000, I'd like to get it back, my queen. I'd like to give him $600,000?

—Oh, very well, very well! Consider it a gift from my empress-self.

A knife was keen to the case, and made all the arrangements, like a great Black World weapon will and could.

—Thank you, and I'll be more attentive to you tonight, my dragon queen!

—That's the spirit. Breaking, crushing, snapping, and ruining those pesky pirates has given me a stunning need to be impaled myself with my husband's angry bludgeoner, and that for a long, long while, and yes, I'll flex mightily all that time for you, I know you worship my Clydesdale-like muscles, is that okay my sweetie-sweet?

I gulped appreciably.

—Just so, my lady!

I said this to the dragoness beneath me, flying back with her, just frustrated with how strongly angelic she seemed, I thought I was in an enlightened and superbly extreme dream.

—My goddess 'n' goodness just behold your esteemed elegance! I'm not trying to express in mere words what my emotions are right now; I really want you to <u>feel</u> what I'm saying to your unestimated grace. You're such a tremendous, dominant, stupendous sight to supremely see! How lucky I am to give pleasure to this immense, she-stallion-like angelic frame, this wonderful, fantastic gem, awesome, amazing and truly astonishing creature that is so high and powerfully above me, you're so lovely! You can be cruel and yet so instantly kind. I'm going up to tremendous, terrific heights with you, just touching you, my definition of glory-gloriousness-godhood! You are a woman, only more so!

And I really, really felt this way about this reptilian too. Everything about her ways, a muscled, enshrined being and it was definitely more than that. I didn't volunteer my evil thoughts, and she didn't insist.

After my little speech, Clare noticeably shook, and responded, half-perplexed, half-laughing, yet all the while, leading up to something titillating. The Lizardanian looked quite vulnerable at this time, her mouth gawking.

—Geez-wow, well, I'm just going to cream myself right here, how dragon-embarrassing for me, but I guess I'll have to get used to this ubiquitous, white-rope-stream (ahem) of words, your being my husband, and all!

—and all, my lady?

—I haven't yet reproduced the ephemeral species (or two), but just give that some time (it <u>is</u> like I'm going to live forever-and-a-night, as you well know, or you ought to). Yes, we'll get to that. I will agree with Soreidian on this point, listening to you is a real nut, I mean, egg-blast!

—Oh, Clare, this has been so glorious, the pixies, the halos, sprites, blue jets and the clouds that looked like, well, just steps—

—You mean Lenticular clouds, with that lens-like appearance? We discovered those, with Black World weapon-help, in Harold's Cross, in Dublin, Ireland?

—It was great flying around it and then through it all, they were so still, it was superb!

—I'm glad you're enjoying it. Almost as good as those Altocumulus clouds over Mount Cook in New Zealand, hey? It was fun flying underneath them, me inverted, with you on my pouting mega-ripped-stomach, right? I think you were looking at my bulbus, suckable abdominals and not the cloud formations overhead, I could tell because you were sucking them raw, slobbering down to my solid obliques? I'm not a suckling mink, but I'm trying to get along with my stallion-like husband.

Hey, that's okay, my abdominals are a Ringling Brothers and Barnum and Bailey kinda Circus, just to make any human beg for more. It was all fun, yes, I'll concede that, rare for a dragon-star! I've seen many worlds' clouds, but that was particularly striking. Ah, yeah, I've been hearing your radio, of late, and I do want to tell you something after I quote a song that Billie Eilish (and her brother, Finneas) sang:

> *As long as I'm here*
> *No one can hurt you*
> *Don't wanna lie here*
> *But you can learn to*
> *If I could change the way that you see yourself*
> *You wouldn't wonder why you're here,*
> *They don't deserve you.*

And that's the main reason I favor you, Brian, and permitted you to evolve into a dragon, too. Humans don't deserve you, you should be a dragon, and, coming with me, that will be your inevitable fate. I do consider it an evolution, making Darwin proud, and you should think so. Or I'll <u>make</u> you think so, draconically. So there, you're with a star dragon now, have some needed respect. Now I'm so strong, mighty, so god-like (and always was) and it's like Billie Eilish said,

> *Cause everybody wants something from me now*
> *And I don't wanna let 'em down.*

Ah yes, that was fun. How do you feel?

—My esteemed lady, I feel fine. What clouds did we see again, Clare?

—Well there were those Lenticular clouds over those Transylvanian mountains, the Arcus, the night shining clouds called Noctilucents, the Fallstreak Holes (you know, the ones they we flew through, the wave clouds, or Fluctus clouds (called the Kelvin-Helmholtz), the cumulonimbus, and the mammatus clouds (you know, those 'mammary,' clouds that we saw over New York City), the cirrus, cumulonimbus and cumulus and then the rainbows, remember?

—Gee, your as smart, as, as, a dragon!

—At least so, my dear!

Something was bothering me, something I had to confess.

—Clare I'm afraid Soreidian was right, and I don't see any way out of it, being a little human as you know I am. By the way, I see a parallel between the Carpenters and Ms. Eilish, and here's what I think: That girl better be careful, I know she's got parents involved in Hollywood, and that's what worries me. The things Soreidian said are mostly right. He said if you give humans anything, then they will want everything, experiencing a huge wealth they always and anyway want something else. You know what Samuel Gompers, the labor leader, thought. "We do want more, and when it becomes more, we shall still want more." I think humans can never get enough, and that just has to do with our limited life-circumstances we just can't control. Forgive us, is all I can think to say. Soreidian was right, in a lot of ways. I still want to make things right with him. You see? We still want just a little more.

Clare was dismissive.

—Don't ask the gods to forgive you; first, you humans should forgive yourselves. As life forms go, you're really not that bad. Ah, Soreidian, he might have a change of heart now, post-football game. Plus, he didn't say all of that.

—Yes, but he meant to say it. And it would all be true, nevertheless. If you give the humans anything, they will need everything, too much for dragon-gods with a small 'g' to even handle. And Clare that's why it's better to be in the clouds, with you, rather than getting famous or listening to the silence, talking to celebrities, and stuff. Chances are they'd just want to get high, and we are, what, 62 miles up, so we—

—That's your 'Thermosphere' mind that, it's also known as the Karman line, remember!

—Yes, my lady, thermosphere, Karman line, the line for outer space. Of course, my serpentine wife, in conclusion, we are high above everyone, and it's just so lovely, as are you, Clare.

After, the swords, knives and hatchets arriving intermittently, we got to see all the clouds and everything on Clare's little bucket list. Clouds looking like 'steps' we most enjoyed, darting in and out, her picturesque dragon wings burning through them. In the end, Clare's weapons won out, referring far more "buckets" than my swords did. Lara showed up, just then, arriving alongside of us, looking splendid and mighty.

—Hey, you guys have a good time?

Clare answered.

—The best, lemme think it to you!

They had a happy telepathy. Lara cooed and looked longingly at me.

—Next time, it's on Alligatoria, I'll show you some extreme stuff, got it, dual-husband? I think Brian's reaching full-animal now, his venial piston, that exquisite truncheon, is indeed smokin' (hot), can we enjoy it later, our magic can make it so gargantuan!

I announced gamely.

—Yes, my dual wife, I love you completely, inside and out!

Lara dithered in the air, her iron wings stalling.

—What was that, human?

—I said I love you inside and out, and I'll stake my life on it, anytime you want. That equally applies to Clare, too!

—Did you hear Clare? He loves us inside and out?

Clare murmured.

—I did hear. Maybe he needs a lesson on what he's really talking about?

—Yeah, hey good idea. I think that little hillock below us will be a great place for a lesson, the one with those trees on it?

They warped down to the little hill, the setting sun, fantastic rays jetting out, warming them.

—Only someone with mighty-might can do what I've got planned. Your weapons are going to participate in our little edification of today's human-husband. Very well, and then some. Brian Miller's weapons come here; hey, where are you going?

They were following the conversation, just floating along at their extreme leisure class, some of the Black World knives were sleeping, the trip was so serine and pleasant. They were rudely awakened.

—Oh, hell to the no!

Lara was angered.

—Tut-and-tut-again-big-league-sword-girl! You will come to order, and that promptly!

The sword whisked away, despite Lara's reaching out to her.

—Wow, you are special! That still won't save you, my little sword, remember that time on the Water World? You will comply and serve me now!

I was aghast, I didn't know what was happening, and I should have.

—What is going on here, Clare, what's the big deal?

—Your statement was.

—Was what?

—A big deal, human.

—Why's that, my esteemed lady?

—Outside and inside?

I was quiet, figuring out where my saurians were going.

Lara whirled around like a ninja, and did snatch one of my hatchets, the one with his soul restored. The hatchet squealed like any old pig pre-butchered.

—You! Hatchet, come here, make an <u>autopsy</u> out of me, pre-postmortem, right now!

Lara was so imperious with her bulky-self, the weapon was still pensive and very frightened. Clare was put-out.

—Oh, me first, Lara, I suggested it!

—Nah-uh, I'm first, I'm a Warlord, almost the strongest saurian ever known, have some deference, Clare!

—No, no, not me I couldn't—

—You will, come here you singularity sprizzler!

—No, no!

My sword intervened.

—I'll do it, please. Release that hatchet Larascena. I'll do it, just like a human autopsy, right? Okay, alright, just stand over next to the tree. Let's just get it over with, geez, I hope you'll appreciate this Brian.

Then, full-realization hit me, and I don't know why it hadn't before.

—You're not going to <u>cut</u> her? I mean, even during the game with the saurians, no one ever came to blows, not even when Danillia knocked the French fries out of that officiating sword after the play was over and—

—I don't have time to hear this old bullshit. You know what to do, I've thought it all to you tardy sword, so just do it! Take a seat Brian, it's not like what you'd think, dumb dummy!

Clare and Lara looked irately over at me, and I shut up. Clare giggled uncontrollably.

—Our human has discovered something, right Clare, and I didn't even have to lean and brutally beat on him, either, bravo Brian!

The autopsy began and my mouth hit the floor, both bigly. Inside a saurian, it wasn't anything like the 'viscera' or 'organs' of a human, oh no. First, no blood 'gushed' fourth. Inside was just a great amount of silver, blues, a little red—really, it looked like a colorful rainbow inside. The blood was there, but it was 'disciplined' blood. And also, inside it was just muscles akimbo and all shining it deep, silver tone. Looking inside them, at the incredible majesty of raw muscle, you could see why number 2 and number 1 was out and out-cold, too. And it pulsed like, well, like it was sexually excited, to put it extremely mildly. I could identify some muscular organs, (many I didn't know, they were a dragon-mystery to me) massively gigantic lungs, sinuous, pulsing inter-abdominals, and a super, massive heart-bulging-muscle. Lara's gigantic pumping organ was silver and beating, no, thrusting vivaciously, hard as any steel. It was just as whopping as my overall chest. I thought it was "organ-esque strapping exquisiteness" the beating titanium, and nuclear weapon defying-ultra-pumper looked really proud to be on such display. The heartbeat reverberated much faster than it did for humans. I had to remember that this heart was eons old, and still looked vital, energetic, vigorous, vivacious and brutally, wholly young. Their tails were equally incredible, wholly (as in 'Holy') vein-ripped-muscle throughout, inside and outside, all massive, physical strength and lucid power.

—What do you think of this internal structure, my slack-jawed Brian? All of this, by the way, can take any weapons that humans care to play with, chemical, nuclear, conventional, anything, just the way my enstrengthened green scales can. I can't see the Justice League with these kinds of internal-muscle-dynamics, right Clare?

—Oh, you said it Lara. Now me, me, autopsy me!

And the reluctant Black World sword did so. Clare was as robust, spirited and dynamic on the inside as Lara was, with a brutal power known only to Lizardanians. Clare's arrangement was much the same as Lara's, only a little bit harder and more vigorous. Her heart was only half the size of Lara's, still huge.

—Come here Brian, don't be shy, touch my heart, feel my awesome, strapping power, step right up on tip-toe, come on.

The saurians drew close together and I managed to touch both brick-iron-pulsing-hearts. It was just like feeling very, very warm steel. Then, they actually flexed, and the amazing hearts beat a lot faster, like a mighty ship's engines at flank speed! Every muscle on the saurians was erect and pleni-potentiary-and-so-prudent right then and ultra-wow and just-them-awe-shucks!

—Goodness, these are very hot, just this side of scalding, just like my ladies!

Both responded, same time.

—Thank you, my child!

With the anti-autopsy thing rectified by magic alone, (it's good to be a dragon-star!) we were fully prepared for our evening 'meal.'

—And now, some magic I've been working on, in anticipation of becoming a dragon, some day. I hope you'll both have me, after I please you. Or if not, and I fail to give you pleasure, don't inquire about me you'll know where I'll be: I'll step off the Golden (ode to 'Billy' again). I've a gift for you, my dears, just call me Two Tongues, and you'll be 'known' by this super, muscular organ, that's for sure. And this isn't an exercise in The Exorcist, and I'm trying to be romantic, I'm sure you understand. I do like scary movies, but that's a personal flaw. Please, let's engage in our ménage a trois. I'm so glad you didn't see that porno-priest horror movie and let's just keep it that way.

I occasioned my queens over. Their scales and fins rose, and I approached them with a reverence, on our famous circular bed. The bed was magically brought from somewhere. I didn't know whose magic was responsible and didn't much care. The stars shined down.

The reptilians didn't know what was going on, but they had their fun in mind. I hadn't disappointed them before, they lay prone, accelerating my potent mouth, until I was covering in their warm, glazing lifewater. I'm not going to talk about my massive pipe-n-piston wrestling matches here with my saurians, my teenager-sheen-and-ultra-goo-explosions. Disappointing in not discussing them, though: It's a glorious, so supreme, so mega-free feeling, my love for these dragonesses: You couldn't go no better. I've explained it elsewhere, so have done.

After many hours, causing my serpents to crest and peak more times than I can tell, covering me with gallons of saurian life-milk, I could feel them both really exhausted (in a great way). Completely satisfied (for now). I didn't even clean myself off; I was clean, clear, and suitably in heaven. Totally enough milked, be sure of that much.

—You know how you can tell you're in 'real love,' my glorious, super-enstrengthened dragonesses, you know what they say?

They murmured, together, in telepathy, both wrapped about our satin sheets in a saurian way.

What do they say?

—"Don't stop." See? That's real, dynamic love! My life has been totally reborn with you both. I'm so humbled and so blessed to be just a small part of your lives. We are all sentient beings, and if loving you is wrong, then wrong I'll be. If anything, uh, untoward, were to happen to either of you, my life would be forfeit, and this life is all I know. You have my life, all of it, and more. That is why the young (and teenagers especially) know what it is to love a dragon-star, and, after that loving, wish death as a separation if they can't have them again and again, *ad infinitum.* You have total, absolute freedom in our marriage, and I encourage this, but I will be true to you in anything I do, before, during and after. I know all my secrets are safe with you and I'd sell my life, gratefully-enough, just set my life at any nappy's pins fee, just to make you supremely happy. That's how I feel! It's okay to talk now. You don't have to genuflect or be embellishing or anything, uh, right, Lara, Clare?

I looked to right and left, after feeling a little ignored.

Unfortunately (or fortunately, you be the judge), they were both soundly asleep. Either way, I saw something shoved over to me: my Water World diamond. Couldn't go no better.

APPENDIX THREE
THE FOOTBALL EXTRAORDINAIRE

Commentators:

Howard Grifford
Frank Facenda
John Maddenhawk
Maddy Kingston (sideline reporter)

Soreidian's Team (Black Fins)

Coached by: Rahabian

Littorian's Team (Green Fins)

Coached by: Kerok

FOOTBALL POSITIONS:

(from Wikipedia, the free encyclopedia, gratefully acknowledged)

PLAYERS:

Valacian (BF)—Ettoros (GF)
Offense: Wide Receiver
Defense: Cornerback

Oriasel (BF)—Direidian (GF)
Offense: Tackle
Defense: Outside Linebacker

Saleosian (BF)—Loridian (GF)
Offense: Guard
Defense: End

Soreidian (BF)—Littorian (GF)
Offense: Center
Defense: Middle Linebacker

Penemuelian (BF)—Terminus (GF)
Offense: Guard
Defense: Tackle

Rachel Dreadnought (BF)—Katrina Chakiaya (GF)
Offense: Quarterback
Defense Substitution: Tackles: Green Team
Israfelian; Black Team, Victorian

Azzaian (BF)—Teresian (GF)
Offense: Safety
Defense: End

Buneian (BF)—Clareina (GF)
Offense: Tight End
Defense: Outside Linebacker

Danillia (BF)—Anakimian (GF)
Offense: Wide Receiver
Defense: Cornerback

Uzzaious (BF)—Korillia (GF)
Offense: Fullback, Tailback, Halfback (Running Back)
Defense: Defensive Tackle

Verrierian —Turinian
Offense: Tackle
Defense: Tackle

APPENDIX FOUR
CLAIR'S BUCKET LIST

1. Aurora: Charged particles from the sun, strike atoms in the Earth's atmosphere. That causes electrons in the atoms to move to a higher-energy level. When the electrons drop back into a lower energy state, they release photons of light.
2. Elves: Emission of Light and Very Low frequency perturbations due to Electromagnetic pulse Sources. Flash of red or purple light.
3. Halo: On top of Elves at 62 miles up, oval shaped.
4. Sprites: Stratospheric Perturbations mesospheric Resulting from Intense Thunderstorm Electrification. Triggered by the discharges of positive lightning between the thundercloud and the ground. Red sprites are at 37 miles up.
5. Meteors: Matter from space entering atmosphere, becoming incandescent as friction appreciating as a streak of light.
6. Gnomes: Different manifestation of blue starters but appear with a more compact shape above convective domes.
7. Pixies: Pinpoints of light, on the surface of convective domes that produce gnomes.

8. Gigantic jets: Initiative between upper positive and lower negative charge regions in a thundercloud. Higher in altitudes that blue jets, and upper portion of the jet changes color from blue to red.

9. Blue jets: Are between six miles and 37 miles up. Ultraviolet emissions from neutral and ionized molecular nitrogen.

10. Noctilucent clouds: Night shining clouds, ice crystals only visible during astronomical twilight (zone).

11. Blue Starters: Upward moving luminous phenomenon closely related to blue jets.

12. Cirrus: Mare's tail appearance, long, fibrous and curved with. No tuffs or curls at the ends.

13. Cumulonimbus: High domed top.

14. Cumulus: Flat dark grey base and tall tower-like formations with tops mostly in the troposphere. Fair weather cloud.

15. Stratocumulus: Lens-shaped low cloud.

16. Double rainbows and triple rainbows: Points to treasure chests at termination, or end, point (when you are with a dragon, that is); green, blue, orange and red, mainly, in a bow-shape visual presentation. And with that, this presentation is done (for now)!

FINIS

Printed in the United States
By Bookmasters